Merry Christmas, Terry.

Grandmom
and
Aunt Doris
'75

48

RIP VAN WINKLE
The LEGEND of
SLEEPY HOLLOW
and Other Tales

Here are four of the most famous stories from the pen of one of the best-loved authors in American literature. Washington Irving traveled and wrote of the folklore of the countries he visited, nearly a hundred and fifty years ago; yet his characters are as fresh and vital today as when they first appeared in print. Who does not know Rip Van Winkle, who slept twenty years on the mountain, only to awake to a whole new world? And that other delightful Hudson River Valley legend, in which Ichabod Crane had his comeuppance from the Headless Horseman of Sleepy Hollow? These and the other exciting stories will bring enjoyment to yet another generation of readers.

RIP VAN WINKLE
The LEGEND of

COMPANION LIBRARY

SLEEPY HOLLOW
and Other Tales

By WASHINGTON IRVING

Illustrations by ROBERTA CARTER CLARK

Grosset & Dunlap

PUBLISHERS   NEW YORK

Contents

Rip Van Winkle   9

The Legend of Sleepy Hollow   45

The Spectre Bridegroom   99

The Moor's Legacy   127

Contents

RIP VAN WINKLE
The LEGEND of SLEEPY HOLLOW
and Other Tales

RIP VAN WINKLE

A Posthumous Writing of
Diedrich Knickerbocker

Preface

THE FOLLOWING TALE was found among the papers of the late Diedrich Knickerbocker, an old gentleman of New York, who was very curious in the Dutch history of the province and the manners of the descendants from its primitive settlers. His historical researches, however, did not lie so much among books as among men; for the former are lamentably scanty on his favorite topics, whereas he found the old burghers, and still more their wives, rich in that legendary lore so invaluable to true history. Whenever, therefore, he happened upon a genuine Dutch family, snugly shut up in its low-roofed farmhouse under a spreading sycamore, he looked upon it as a little clasped volume of black-letter, and studied it with the zeal of a bookworm.

PREFACE** 11**

The result of all these researches was a history
of the province during the reign of the Dutch
governors, which he published some years since.
There have been various opinions as to the literary
character of his work, and, to tell the truth, it is
not a whit better than it should be. Its chief merit
is its scrupulous accuracy, which indeed was a
little questioned on its first appearance, but has
since been completely established; and it is now
admitted into all historical collections as a book of
unquestionable authority.

The old gentleman died shortly after the publi-
cation of his work, and now that he is dead and
gone, it cannot do much harm to his memory to
say that his time might have been much better
employed in weightier labors. He, however, was
apt to ride his hobby his own way; and though
it did now and then kick up the dust a little in the
eyes of his neighbors, and grieve the spirit of some
friends for whom he felt the truest deference and
affection, yet his errors and follies are remembered
"more in sorrow than in anger," and it begins to
be suspected that he never intended to injure or
offend. But, however his memory may be appreci-
ated by critics, it is still held dear by many folk
whose good opinion is well worth having; particularly by certain biscuit-bakers, who have gone so
far as to imprint his likeness on their New Year
cakes, and have thus given him a chance for im-
mortality almost equal to the being stamped on a
Waterloo medal or a Queen Anne's farthing.

By Woden, God of Saxons,
From whence comes Wensday, that is Wodensday.

Truth is a thing that ever I will keep
Unto thylke day in which i Creepe into

My sepulchre—

CARTWRIGHT

RIP VAN WINKLE

WHOEVER HAS MADE a voyage up the Hudson must remember the Kaatskill Mountains. They are a dismembered branch of the great Appalachian family, and are seen away to the west of the river, swelling up to a noble height, and lording it over the surrounding country. Every change of season, every change of weather, indeed, every hour of the day produces some change in the magical hues and shapes of these mountains; and they are regarded by all the good wives, far and near, as perfect barometers. When the weather is fair and settled, they are clothed in blue and purple, and print their bold outlines on the clear evening sky; but sometimes, when the rest of the landscape is cloudless, they will gather a hood of gray vapors about their summits, which,

in the last rays of the setting sun, will glow and
light up like a crown of glory.

At the foot of these fairy mountains, the voyager
may have descried the light smoke curling up
from a village, whose shingle roofs gleam among
the trees just where the blue tints of the upland
melt away into the fresh green of the nearer landscape. It is a little village of great antiquity,
having been founded by some of the Dutch
colonists in the early times of the province, just
about the beginning of the government of the good
Peter Stuyvesant (may he rest in peace!) and
there were some of the houses of the original
settlers standing within a few years, built of small
yellow bricks brought from Holland, having lat-
ticed windows and gable fronts, surmounted with
weathercocks.

In that same village, and in one of these very
houses (which, to tell the precise truth, was sadly
timeworn and weatherbeaten) there lived, many
years since, while the country was yet a province
of Great Britain, a simple, good-natured fellow, of
the name of Rip Van Winkle. He was a descendant of the Van Winkles who figured so gallantly
in the chivalrous days of Peter Stuyvesant and
accompanied him to the siege of Fort Christina.
He inherited, however, but little of the martial
character of his ancestors. I have observed that he
was a simple, good-natured man; he was, moreover, a kind neighbor and an obedient, henpecked
husband. Indeed, to the latter circumstance might

be owing that meekness of spirit which gained him
such universal popularity; for those men are apt
to be obsequious and conciliating abroad, who are
under the discipline of shrews at home. Their
tempers, doubtless, are rendered pliant and mal-
leable in the fiery furnace of domestic tribulation,
and a curtain lecture is worth all the sermons in
the world for teaching the virtues of patience and
long-suffering. A termagant wife may, therefore, in
some respects, be considered a tolerable blessing,
and if so, Rip Van Winkle was thrice blessed.

Certain it is, that he was a great favorite among
all the good wives of the village, who, as usual
with the amiable sex, took his part in all family
squabbles, and never failed, whenever they talked
those matters over in their evening gossipings, to
lay all the blame on Dame Van Winkle. The
children of the village, too, would shout with joy
whenever he approached. He assisted at their
sports, made their playthings, taught them to fly
kites and shoot marbles, and told them long
stories of ghosts, witches, and Indians. Whenever
he went dodging about the village, he was surrounded by a troop of them hanging on his skirts,
clambering on his back, and playing a thousand
tricks on him with impunity; and not a dog would
bark at him throughout the neighborhood.

The great error in Rip's composition was an in-
superable aversion to all kinds of profitable labor.
It could not be from the want of assiduity or perseverance; for he would sit on a wet rock, with a

rod as long and heavy as a Tartar's lance, and fish all day without a murmur, even though he should not be encouraged by a single nibble. He would carry a fowling-piece on his shoulder for hours together, trudging through woods and swamps, and up hill and down dale, to shoot a few squirrels or wild pigeons. He would never refuse to assist a neighbor even in the roughest toil, and was a foremost man at all county frolics for husking Indian corn, or building stone fences; the women of the village, too, used to employ him to run their errands, and to do such little odd jobs as their less obliging husbands would not do for them. In a word, Rip was ready to attend to anybody's business but his own; but as to doing family duty and keeping his farm in order, he found it impossible.

In fact, he declared it was of no use to work on his farm; it was the most pestilent little piece of ground in the whole country; everything about it went wrong, and would go wrong in spite of him. His fences were continually falling to pieces; his cow would either go astray, or get among the cabbages; weeds were sure to grow quicker in his fields than anywhere else; the rain always made a point of setting in just as he had some outdoor work to do; so that though his patrimonial estate had dwindled away under his management, acre by acre, until there was little more left than a mere patch of Indian corn and potatoes, yet it was the worst-conditioned farm in the neighborhood.

His children, too, were as ragged and wild as if

they belonged to nobody. His son Rip, an urchin begotten in his own likeness, promised to inherit the habits, with the old clothes, of his father. He was generally seen trooping like a colt at his mother's heels, equipped in a pair of his father's cast-off galli-gaskins which he had much ado to hold up with one hand, as a fine lady does her train in bad weather.

Rip Van Winkle, however, was one of those happy mortals, of foolish, well-oiled dispositions, who take the world easy, eat white bread or brown, whichever can be got with least thought or trouble, and would rather starve on a penny than work for a pound. If left to himself, he would have whistled life away, in perfect contentment; but his wife kept continually dinning in his ears about his idleness, his carelessness, and the ruin he was bringing on his family. Morning, noon, and night, her tongue was incessantly going, and everything he said or did was sure to produce a torrent of household eloquence. Rip had but one way of replying to all lectures of the kind, and that, by frequent use, had grown into a habit. He shrugged his shoulders, shook his head, cast up his eyes, but said nothing. This, however, always provoked a fresh volley from his wife, so that he was fain to draw off his forces, and take to the outside of the house—the only side which, in truth, belongs to a henpecked husband.

Rip's sole domestic adherent was his dog Wolf, who was as much henpecked as his master; for

Dame Van Winkle regarded them as companions
in idleness, and even looked upon Wolf with an
evil eye as the cause of his master's going so often
astray. True it is, in all points of spirit befitting an
honorable dog, he was as courageous an animal
as ever scoured the woods—but what courage can
withstand the ever-doing and all-besetting terrors of a woman's tongue? The moment Wolf
entered the house, his crest fell, his tail drooped
to the ground, or curled between his legs, he
sneaked about with a gallows air, casting many a
sidelong glance at Dame Van Winkle, and at the
least flourish of a broomstick or ladle, he would
fly to the door with yelping precipitation.

Times grew worse and worse with Rip Van
Winkle as years of matrimony rolled on; a tart
temper never mellows with age, and a sharp
tongue is the only edged tool that grows keener
with constant use. For a long while he used to
console himself, when driven from home, by fre-
quenting a kind of perpetual club of the sages,
philosophers, and other idle personages of the
village, which held its sessions on a bench before
a small inn, designated by a rubicund portrait
of His Majesty George the Third. Here they used
to sit in the shade through a long, lazy summer's
day, talking listlessly over village gossip, or telling
endless, sleepy stories about nothing. But it
would have been worth any statesman's money to
have heard the profound discussions which sometimes took place, when by chance an old news-

paper fell into their hands from some passing traveler. How solemnly they would listen to the contents, as drawled out by Derrick Van Brummel, the schoolmaster, a dapper, learned little man, who was not to be daunted by the most gigantic word in the dictionary; and how sagely they would deliberate upon public events some months after they had taken place.

The opinions of this junto were completely controlled by Nicholas Vedder, a patriarch of the village and landlord of the inn, at the door of which he took his seat from morning till night, just moving sufficiently to avoid the sun, and keep in the shade of a large tree; so that the neighbors could tell the hour by his movements as accurately as by a sundial. It is true, he was rarely heard to speak, but smoked his pipe incessantly. His adherents, however (for every great man has his adherents), perfectly understood him, and knew how to gather his opinions. When anything that was read or related displeased him, he was observed to smoke his pipe vehemently, and to send forth short, frequent, and angry puffs; but when pleased, he would inhale the smoke slowly and tranquilly, and emit it in light and placid clouds, and sometimes, taking the pipe from his mouth and letting the fragrant vapor curl about his nose, would gravely nod his head in token of perfect approbation.

From even this stronghold the unlucky Rip was at length routed by his termagant wife, who

would suddenly break in upon the tranquility of
the assemblage, and call the members all to
nought; nor was that august personage, Nicholas
Vedder himself, sacred from the daring tongue of
this terrible virago, who charged him outright with
encouraging her husband in habits of idleness.

Poor Rip was at last reduced almost to despair;
and his only alternative, to escape from the labor
of the farm and the clamor of his wife, was to take
a gun in hand, and stroll away into the woods.
Here he would sometimes seat himself at the foot
of a tree, and share the contents of his wallet with
Wolf, with whom he sympathized as a fellow-suf-
ferer in persecution. "Poor Wolf," he would say,
"thy mistress leads thee a dog's life of it; but never
mind, my lad, whilst I live thou shalt never want
a friend to stand by thee!" Wolf would wag his
tail, look wistfully in his master's face, and if dogs
can feel pity, I verily believe he reciprocated the
sentiment with all his heart.

In a long ramble of the kind, on a fine autumnal
day, Rip had unconsciously scrambled to one of
the highest parts of the Kaatskill Mountains. He
was after his favorite sport of squirrel-shooting,
and the still solitudes had echoed and re-echoed
with the reports of his gun. Panting and fatigued,
he threw himself, late in the afternoon, on a green
knoll, covered with mountain herbage, that
crowned the brow of a precipice. From an opening between the trees he could overlook all the
lower country for many a mile of rich woodland.

He saw at a distance the lordly Hudson, far, far below him, moving on its silent but majestic course, with the reflection of a purple cloud or the sail of a lagging bark here and there sleeping on its glassy bosom, and at last losing itself in the blue highlands.

On the other side he looked down into a deep mountain glen, wild, lonely, and shagged, the bottom filled with fragments from the impending cliffs, and scarcely lighted by the reflected rays of the setting sun. For some time Rip lay musing on this scene; evening was gradually advancing; the mountains began to throw their long blue shadows over the valleys; he saw that it would be dark long before he could reach the village; and he heaved a heavy sigh when he thought of encountering the terrors of Dame Van Winkle.

As he was about to descend, he heard a voice from a distance hallooing: "Rip Van Winkle! Rip Van Winkle!" He looked around, but could see nothing but a crow winging its solitary flight across the mountain. He thought his fancy must have deceived him, and turned again to descend, when he heard the same cry ring through the still, evening air, "Rip Van Winkle! Rip Van Winkle!" —at the same time Wolf bristled up his back, and giving a low growl, skulked to his master's side, looking fearfully down into the glen. Rip now felt a vague apprehension stealing over him; he looked anxiously in the same direction, and perceived a strange figure slowly toiling up the rocks, and

bending under the weight of something he carried on his back. He was surprised to see any
human being in this lonely and unfrequented
place, but supposing it to be someone of the
neighborhood in need of his assistance, he hastened down to yield it.

On nearer approach, he was still more surprised
at the singularity of the stranger's appearance. He
was a short, square-built old fellow, with thick
bushy hair, and a grizzled beard. His dress was of
the antique Dutch fashion—a cloth jerkin strapped
round the waist—several pairs of breeches, the
outer one of ample volume, decorated with rows
of buttons down the sides, and bunches at the
knees. He bore on his shoulders a stout keg, that
seemed full of liquor, and made signs for Rip to
approach and assist him with the load. Though
rather shy and distrustful of this new acquaintance, Rip complied with his usual alacrity; and
mutually relieving each other, they clambered up
a narrow gully, apparently the dry bed of a
mountain torrent. As they ascended, Rip every
now and then heard long rolling peals, like
distant thunder, that seemed to issue out of a
deep ravine, or rather cleft between lofty rocks,
toward which their rugged path conducted.
He paused for an instant, but supposing it to be
the muttering of one of those transient thunder-
showers which often take place in the mountain heights, he proceeded. Passing through the
ravine, they came to a hollow, like a small amphi-

theatre, surrounded by perpendicular precipices, over the brinks of which impending trees shot their branches, so that you only caught glimpses of the azure sky, and the bright evening cloud. During the whole time Rip and his companion had labored on in silence; for though the former marveled greatly what could be the object of carrying a keg of liquor up this wild mountain, yet there was something strange and incomprehensible about the unknown, that inspired awe and checked familiarity.

On entering the amphitheatre, new objects of wonder presented themselves. On a level spot in the center was a company of odd-looking personages playing at ninepins. They were dressed in quaint outlandish fashion; some wore short doublets, others jerkins, with long knives in their belts, and most of them had enormous breeches, of similar style with that of the guide's. Their visages, too, were peculiar; one had a large head, broad face, and small piggish eyes; the face of another seemed to consist entirely of nose, and was surmounted by a white sugar-loaf hat, set off with a little red cock's tail. They all had beards, of various shapes and colors. There was one who seemed to be the commander. He was a stout old gentleman, with a weatherbeaten countenance; he wore a laced doublet, broad belt and hanger, high-crowned hat and feather, red stockings, and high-heeled shoes with roses on them. The whole group reminded Rip of the figures in an old Flemish

Nothing interrupted the stillness of the scene but the noise of the balls

painting, in the parlor of Dominie Van Shaick, the village parson, and which had been brought over from Holland at the time of the settlement.

What seemed particularly odd to Rip was, that though these folks were evidently amusing themselves, yet they maintained the gravest faces, the most mysterious silence, and were, withal, the most melancholy party of pleasure he had ever witnessed. Nothing interrupted the stillness of the scene but the noise of the balls, which, whenever they were rolled, echoed along the mountains like rumbling peals of thunder.

As Rip and his companion approached them they suddenly desisted from their play, and stared at him with such fixed statue-like gaze, and such strange, uncouth, lack-lustre countenances, that his heart turned within him, and his knees smote together. His companion now emptied the contents of the keg into large flagons, and made signs to him to wait upon the company. He obeyed with fear and trembling; they quaffed the liquor in profound silence, and then returned to their game.

By degrees, Rip's awe and apprehension subsided. He even ventured, when no eye was fixed upon him, to taste the beverage, which he found had much of the flavor of excellent Hollands. He was naturally a thirsty soul, and was soon tempted to repeat the draft. One taste provoked another; and he reiterated his visits to the flagon so often that at length his senses were overpowered, his eyes swam in his head, his head gradually declined, and he fell into a deep sleep.

On waking, he found himself on the green knoll
whence he had first seen the old man of the glen.
He rubbed his eyes—it was a bright sunny morning. The birds were hopping and twittering among
the bushes, and the eagle was wheeling aloft, and
breasting the pure mountain breeze. "Surely,"
thought Rip, "I have not slept here all night." He
recalled the occurrences before he fell asleep. The
strange man with the keg of liquor—the mountain
ravine—the wild retreat among the rocks—the
woebegone party at ninepins—the flagon.

"Oh, that flagon! That wicked flagon!" thought
Rip—"What excuse shall I make to Dame Van
Winkle?"

He looked round for his gun, but in place of the
clean, well-oiled fowling-piece, he found an old
firelock lying by him, the barrel incrusted with
rust, the lock falling off, and the stock worm-eaten.
He now suspected that the grave roisterers of the
mountain had put a trick upon him, and having
dosed him with liquor, had robbed him of his gun.
Wolf, too, had disappeared, but he might have
strayed away after a squirrel or partridge. He
whistled after him and shouted his name, but all
in vain; the echoes repeated his whistle and shout,
but no dog was to be seen.

He determined to revisit the scene of the last
evening's gambol, and if he met with any of the
party, to demand his dog and gun. As he rose to
walk, he found himself stiff in the joints, and want-
ing in his usual activity. "These mountain beds

do not agree with me," thought Rip, "and if this frolic should lay me up with a fit of rheumatism, I shall have a blessed time with Dame Van Winkle." With some difficulty he got down into the glen; he found the gully up which he and his companion had ascended the preceding evening; but to his astonishment a mountain stream was now foaming down it, leaping from rock to rock, and filling the glen with babbling murmurs. He, however, made shift to scramble up its sides, working his toilsome way through thickets of birch, sassafras, and witch hazel; and sometimes tripped up or entangled by the wild grapevines that twisted their coils or tendrils from tree to tree, and spread a kind of network in his path.

At length he reached to where the ravine had opened through the cliffs to the amphitheatre; but no traces of such opening remained. The rocks presented a high impenetrable wall, over which the torrent came tumbling in a sheet of feathery foam, and fell into a broad deep basin, black from the shadows of the surrounding forest. Here, then, poor Rip was brought to a stand. He again called and whistled after his dog; he was only answered by the cawing of a flock of idle crows, sporting high in the air about a dry tree that overhung a sunny precipice; and who, secure in their elevation, seemed to look down and scoff at the poor man's perplexities. What was to be done? The morning was passing away, and Rip felt famished for want of his breakfast. He grieved to give up his

28 RIP VAN WINKLE

dog and gun; he dreaded to meet his wife; but it
would not do to starve among the mountains. He
shook his head, shouldered the rusty firelock,
and, with a heart full of trouble and anxiety,
turned his steps homeward.

As he approached the village, he met a number
of people, but none whom he knew, which somewhat surprised him, for he had thought himself
acquainted with everyone in the country round.
Their dress, too, was of a different fashion from
that to which he was accustomed. They all stared
at him with equal marks of surprise, and whenever they cast their eyes upon him, invariably
stroked their chins. The constant recurrence of this
gesture induced Rip, involuntarily, to do the
same, when, to his astonishment, he found his
beard had grown a foot long!

He had now entered the skirts of the village.
A troop of strange children ran at his heels, hooting after him, and pointing at his gray beard.
The dogs, too, not one of which he recognized for
an old acquaintance, barked at him as he passed.
The very village was altered: it was larger and
more populous. There were rows of houses which
he had never seen before, and those which had
been his familiar haunts had disappeared. Strange
names were over the doors—strange faces at the
windows—everything was strange. His mind now
misgave him; he began to doubt whether both he
and the world around him were not bewitched.
Surely this was his native village, which he had

left but the day before. There stood the Kaatskill Mountains—there ran the silver Hudson at a distance—there was every hill and dale precisely as it had always been—Rip was sorely perplexed— "That flagon last night," thought he, "has addled my poor head sadly!"

It was with some difficulty that he found the way to his own house, which he approached with silent awe, expecting every moment to hear the shrill voice of Dame Van Winkle. He found the house gone to decay—the roof fallen in, the windows shattered, and the doors off the hinges. A half-starved dog, that looked like Wolf, was skulking about it. Rip called him by name, but the cur snarled, showed his teeth, and passed on. This was an unkind cut indeed. "My very dog," sighed poor Rip, "has forgotten me!"

He entered the house, which, to tell the truth, Dame Van Winkle had always kept in neat order. It was empty, forlorn, and apparently abandoned. This desolateness overcame all his connubial fears —he called loudly for his wife and children—the lonely chambers rang for a moment with his voice, and then all again was silence.

He now hurried forth, and hastened to his old resort, the village inn—but it, too, was gone. A large rickety wooden building stood in its place, with great gaping windows, some of them broken, and mended with old hats and petticoats, and over the door was painted, "The Union Hotel, by Jonathan Doolittle." Instead of the great tree

that used to shelter the quiet little Dutch inn of
yore, there now was reared a tall naked pole, with
something on the top that looked like a red night-
cap, and from it was fluttering a flag, on which
was a singular assemblage of stars and stripes—
all this was strange and incomprehensible. He
recognized on the sign, however, the ruby face of
King George, under which he had smoked so
many a peaceful pipe, but even this was singularly
metamorphosed. The red coat was changed for
one of blue and buff, a sword was held in the
hand instead of a sceptre, the head was decorated
with a cocked hat, and underneath was painted
in large characters, "GENERAL WASHINGTON."

There was, as usual, a crowd of folk about the
door, but none that Rip recollected. The very
character of the people seemed changed. There
was a busy, bustling, disputatious tone about it,
instead of the accustomed phlegm and drowsy
tranquility. He looked in vain for the sage Nicholas Vedder, with his broad face, double chin, and
fair long pipe, uttering clouds of tobacco smoke,
instead of idle speeches; or Van Brummel, the
schoolmaster, doling forth the contents of an ancient newspaper. In place of these, a lean, bilious-
looking fellow, with his pockets full of handbills,
was haranguing vehemently about rights of citi-
zens—elections—members of Congress—liberty
—Bunker's Hill—heroes of seventy-six—and other
words, which were a perfect Babylonish jargon to
the bewildered Van Winkle.

The appearance of Rip, with his long, grizzled beard, his rusty fowling-piece, his uncouth dress, and an army of women and children at his heels, soon attracted the attention of the tavern politicians. They crowded round him, eyeing him from head to foot with great curiosity. The orator bustled up to him, and drawing him partly aside, inquired, "on which side he voted?" Rip stared in vacant stupidity. Another short but busy little fellow pulled him by the arm, and rising on tiptoe, inquired in his ear, "whether he was Federal or Democrat." Rip was equally at a loss to comprehend the question; when a knowing, self-important old gentleman, in a sharp cocked hat, made his way through the crowd, putting them to the right and left with his elbows as he passed, and planting himself before Van Winkle, with one arm akimbo, the other resting on his cane, his keen eyes and sharp hat penetrating, as it were, into his very soul, demanded in an austere tone, "What brought him to the election with a gun on his shoulder, and a mob at his heels; and whether he meant to breed a riot in the village?"

"Alas, gentlemen!" cried Rip, somewhat dismayed, "I am a poor, quiet man, a native of the place, and a loyal subject of the King, God bless him!"

Here a general shout burst from the bystanders —"A tory! A tory! A spy! A refugee! Hustle him! Away with him!" It was with great difficulty that the self-important man in the cocked hat restored

"Alas, gentlemen!" cried Rip, *"I am a loyal subject of the King!"*

order; and having assumed a tenfold austerity of brow, demanded again of the unknown culprit what he came there for, and whom he was seeking. The poor man humbly assured him that he meant no harm, but merely came there in search of some of his neighbors, who used to keep about the tavern.

"Well—who are they? Name them."

Rip bethought himself a moment, and inquired, "Where's Nicholas Vedder?"

There was a silence for a little while, when an old man replied, in a thin, piping voice, "Nicholas Vedder? Why, he is dead and gone these eighteen years. There was a wooden tombstone in the churchyard that used to tell all about him, but that's rotten and gone, too."

"Where's Brom Dutcher?"

"Oh, he went off to the army in the beginning of the war; some say he was killed at the storming of Stony Point—others say he was drowned in a squall at the foot of Antony's Nose. I don't know— he never came back again."

"Where's Van Brummel, the schoolmaster?"

"He went off to the wars, too; was a great militia general, and is now in Congress."

Rip's heart died away, at hearing of these sad changes in his home and friends, and finding himself thus alone in the world. Every answer puzzled him, too, by treating of such enormous lapses of time, and of matters which he could not understand: war—Congress—Stony Point—he had no courage to ask after any more friends, but cried out in despair, "Does nobody here know Rip Van Winkle?"

"Oh, Rip Van Winkle" exclaimed two or three. "Oh, to be sure! That's Rip Van Winkle yonder, leaning against the tree."

Rip looked, and beheld a precise counterpart of himself as he went up the mountain; apparently as lazy, and certainly as ragged. The poor fellow was now completely confounded. He doubted his own identity, and whether he was himself or another man. In the midst of his bewilderment, the man in the cocked hat demanded who he was, and what was his name?

"God knows!" exclaimed he at his wit's end. "I'm not myself—I'm somebody else—that's me yonder —no—that's somebody else, got into my shoes—I was myself last night, but I fell asleep on the mountains, and they've changed my gun, and everything's changed, and I'm changed, and I can't tell what's my name, or who I am!"

The bystanders began now to look at each other, nod, wink significantly, and tap their fingers against their foreheads. There was a whisper, also, about securing the gun, and keeping the old fellow from doing mischief; at the very suggestion of which, the self-important man with the cocked hat retired with some precipitation. At this critical moment a fresh, comely woman pressed through the throng to get a peep at the gray-bearded man. She had a chubby child in her arms, which, frightened at his looks, began to cry. "Hush, Rip," cried she, "hush, you little fool; the old man won't hurt you." The name of the child, the air of the mother, the tone of her voice, all awakened a train of recollections in his mind.

"What is your name, my good woman?" asked he.

"Judith Gardenier."

"And your father's name?"

"Ah, poor man, Rip Van Winkle was his name, but it's twenty years since he went away from home with his gun, and never has been heard of since—his dog came home without him; but whether he shot himself, or was carried away by the Indians, nobody can tell. I was then but a little girl."

Rip had but one more question to ask; but he put it with a faltering voice:

"Where's your mother?"

Oh, she, too, had died but a short time since; she broke a blood-vessel in a fit of passion at a New England peddler.

There was a drop of comfort, at least, in this intelligence. The honest man could contain himself no longer. He caught his daughter and her child in his arms. "I am your father!" cried he— "Young Rip Van Winkle once—old Rip Van Winkle now—Does nobody know poor Rip Van Winkle!"

All stood amazed, until an old woman, tottering out from among the crowd, put her hand to

her brow, and peering under it in his face for a
moment exclaimed, "Sure enough! It is Rip Van
Winkle—it is himself. Welcome home again, old
neighbor. Why, where have you been all these
twenty long years?"

Rip's story was soon told, for the whole twenty
years had been to him but as one night. The
neighbors stared when they heard it; some were
seen to wink at each other, and put their tongues
in their cheeks; and the self-important man in the
cocked hat, who, when the alarm was over, had
returned to the field, screwed down the corners of
his mouth, and shook his head—upon which there
was a general shaking of the head throughout the
assemblage.

It was determined, however, to take the opinion
of old Peter Vanderdonk, who was seen slowly advancing up the road. He was a descendant of
the historian of that name, who wrote one of the
earliest accounts of the province. Peter was the
most ancient inhabitant of the village, and well
versed in all the wonderful events and traditions
of the neighborhood. He recollected Rip at once,
and corroborated his story in the most satisfactory
manner. He assured the company that it was
a fact, handed down from his ancestor, the historian, that the Kaatskill Mountains had always
been haunted by strange beings. That it was affirmed that the great Hendrick Hudson, the first
discoverer of the river and country, kept a kind of
vigil there every twenty years, with his crew of

the Halfmoon; being permitted in this way to revisit the scenes of his enterprise, and keep a
guardian eye upon the river and the great city
called by his name. That his father had once seen
them in their old Dutch dresses playing at ninepins in a hollow of the mountain; and that he
himself had heard, one summer afternoon, the
sound of their balls, like distant peals of thunder.

To make a long story short, the company broke
up, and returned to the more important concerns
of the election. Rip's daughter took him home to
live with her; she had a snug, well-furnished
house, and a stout, cheery farmer for a husband,
whom Rip recollected for one of the urchins that
used to climb upon his back. As to Rip's son and
heir, who was the ditto of himself, seen leaning
against the tree, he was employed to work on the
farm; but evinced an hereditary disposition to
attend to anything else but his business.

Rip now resumed his old walks and habits; he
soon found many of his former cronies, though all
rather the worse for the wear and tear of time;
and preferred making friends among the rising
generation, with whom he soon grew into great
favor.

Having nothing to do at home, and being arrived at that happy age when a man can be idle
with impunity, he took his place once more on
the bench at the inn door, and was reverenced as
one of the patriarchs of the village, and a chroni-
cler of the old times "before the war." It was some

time before he could get into the regular track of
gossip, or could be made to comprehend the
strange events that had taken place during his
torpor. How that there had been a Revolutionary
War—that the country had thrown off the yoke of
old England—and that, instead of being a subject
of His Majesty George the Third, he was now a
free citizen of the United States. Rip, in fact, was
no politician; the changes of states and empires
made but little impression on him; but there was
one species of despotism under which he had long
groaned, and that was—petticoat government.
Happily, that was at an end; he had got his neck
out of the yoke of matrimony, and could go in and
out whenever he pleased without dreading the
tyranny of Dame Van Winkle. Whenever her
name was mentioned, however, he shook his
head, shrugged his shoulders, and cast up his
eyes; which might pass either for an expression of
resignation to his fate, or joy at his deliverance.

He used to tell his story to every stranger that
arrived at Mr. Doolittle's hotel. He was observed,
at first, to vary on some points every time he told
it, which was, doubtless, owing to his having so
recently awaked. It at last settled down precisely
to the tale I have related, and not a man, woman,
or child in the neighborhood, but knew it by
heart. Some always pretended to doubt the reality
of it, and insisted that Rip had been out of his
head, and that this was one point on which he always remained flighty. The old Dutch inhabitants,

however, almost universally gave it full credit. Even to this day, they never hear a thunderstorm of a summer afternoon about the Kaatskill, but they say Hendrick Hudson and his crew are at their game of ninepins; and it is a common wish of all henpecked husbands in the neighborhood, when life hangs heavy on their hands, that they might have a quieting draft out of Rip Van Winkle's flagon.

Note

The foregoing tale, one would suspect, had been suggested to Mr. Knickerbocker by a little German superstition about the Emperor Frederick der Rothbart and the Kypphauser mountain; the subjoined note, however, which he had appended to the tale, shows that it is an absolute fact, narrated with his usual fidelity.

"The story of Rip Van Winkle may seem incredible to many, but nevertheless I give it my full belief, for I know the vicinity of our old Dutch settlements to have been very subject to marvelous events and appearances. Indeed, I have heard many stranger stories than this in the villages along the Hudson; all of which were too well authenticated to admit of a doubt. I have even talked with Rip Van Winkle myself, who, when last I saw him, was a venerable old man, and so perfectly rational and consistent on every other point, that I think no conscientious person could refuse to take this into the bargain; nay, I have seen a certificate on the subject taken before a country justice, and signed with a cross in the justice's own handwriting. The story, therefore, is beyond the possibility of doubt.

"D. K."

Postscript

The following are traveling notes from a memo-randum book of Mr. Knickerbocker:

The Kaatsberg or Catskill mountains have al-ways been a region full of fable. The Indians con-sidered them the abode of spirits who influenced the weather, spreading sunshine or clouds over the landscape, and sending good or bad hunting seasons. They were ruled by an old squaw spirit, said to be their mother. She dwelled on the highest peak of the Catskills, and had charge of the doors of day and night, to open and shut them at the proper hour. She hung up the new moons in the skies, and cut up the old ones into stars. In times of drought, if properly propitiated, she would spin light summer clouds out of cobwebs and morning dew, and send them off from the crest of the

mountain, flake after flake, like flakes of carded
cotton, to float in the air; until, dissolved by the
heat of the sun, they would fall in gentle showers,
causing the grass to spring, the fruits to ripen, and
the corn to grow an inch an hour. If displeased,
however, she would brew up clouds black as ink,
sitting in the midst of them like a bottle-bellied
spider in the midst of its web; and when these
clouds broke, woe betide the valleys!

In old times, say the Indian traditions, there
was a kind of Manitou or Spirit, who kept about
the wildest recesses of the Catskill mountains, and
took a mischievous pleasure in wreaking all kinds
of evils and vexations upon the red men. Sometimes he would assume the form of a bear, a
panther, or a deer, lead the bewildered hunter a
weary chase through tangled forests and among
ragged rocks, and then spring off with a loud ho!
ho! leaving him aghast on the brink of a beetling
precipice or raging torrent.

The favorite abode of this Manitou is still
shown. It is a great rock or cliff on the loneliest
part of the mountains, and, from the flowering
vines which clamber about it, and the wild flowers
which abound in its neighborhood, is known by
the name of the Garden Rock. Near the foot of it is
a small lake, the haunt of the solitary bittern, with
water snakes basking in the sun on the leaves of
the pond lilies which lie on the surface. This place
was held in great awe by the Indians, insomuch
that the boldest hunter would not pursue his game

within its precincts. Once upon a time, however, a hunter who had lost his way penetrated to the Garden Rock, where he beheld a number of gourds placed in the crotches of trees. One of these he seized and made off with it, but in the hurry of his retreat he let it fall among the rocks, when a great stream gushed forth which washed him away and swept him down precipices, where he was dashed to pieces, and the stream made its way to the Hudson, and continues to flow to the present day, being the identical stream known by the name of the Kaaterskill.

The LEGEND of SLEEPY HOLLOW

*Found among the Papers of the Late
Diedrich Knickerbocker*

A pleasing land of Drowsy Head it was,
　Of dreams that wave before the half-shut eye,
And of gay castles in the clouds that pass,
　Forever flushing round a summer sky.

CASTLE OF INDOLENCE

The LEGEND of
SLEEPY HOLLOW

IN THE BOSOM of one of those
spacious coves which indent the eastern shore of
the Hudson, at that broad expansion of the river
denominated by the ancient Dutch navigators the
Tappan Zee, and where they always prudently
shortened sail and implored the protection of St.
Nicholas when they crossed, there lies a small
market town or rural port, which by some is called
Greensburg, but which is more generally and
properly known by the name of Tarry Town. This
name was given, we are told, in former days by
the good housewives of the adjacent country from
the inveterate propensity of their husbands to
linger about the village tavern on market days. Be
that as it may, I do not vouch for the fact, but
merely advert to it for the sake of being precise

and authentic. Not far from this village, perhaps about two miles, there is a little valley, or rather lap of land, among high hills, which is one of the quietest places in the whole world. A small brook glides through it, with just murmur enough to lull one to repose, and the occasional whistle of a quail or tapping of a woodpecker are almost the only sounds that ever break in upon the uniform tranquility.

I recollect that, when a stripling, my first exploit in squirrel-shooting was in a grove of tall walnut trees that shades one side of the valley. I had wandered into it at noontime, when all Nature is peculiarly quiet, and was startled by the roar of my own gun as it broke the Sabbath stillness around and was prolonged and reverberated by the angry echoes. If ever I should wish for a retreat whither I might steal from the world and its distractions and dream quietly away the remnant of a troubled life, I know of none more promising than this little valley.

From the listless repose of the place and the peculiar character of its inhabitants, who are descendants from the original Dutch settlers, this sequestered glen has long been known by the name of Sleepy Hollow, and its rustic lads are called the Sleepy Hollow Boys throughout all the neighboring country. A drowsy, dreamy influence seems to hang over the land and to pervade the very atmosphere. Some say that the place was bewitched by a High German doctor during the early days of the settlement; others that an old Indian chief, the prophet or wizard of his tribe, held his powwows there before the country was discovered by Master Hendrick Hudson. Certain it is, the place still continues under the sway of some witching power that holds a spell over the minds of the good people, causing them to walk in a continual reverie. They are given to all kinds of marvelous beliefs, are subject to trances and visions, and frequently see strange sights and hear music and voices in the air. The whole neighborhood abounds with local tales, haunted spots, and twilight superstition; stars shoot and meteors glare oftener across the valley than in any other part of the country; and the nightmare, with her whole ninefold, seems to make it the favorite scene of her gambols.

The dominant spirit, however, that haunts this enchanted region, and seems to be commander-in-chief of all the powers of the air, is the apparition of a figure on horseback without a head. It is said by some to be the ghost of a Hessian trooper whose head had been carried away by a cannonball in some nameless battle during the Revolutionary War, and who is, ever and anon, seen by the country folk hurrying along in the gloom of night as if on the wings of the wind. His haunts are not confined to the valley, but extend at times to the adjacent roads, and especially to the vicinity of a church at no great distance. Indeed, certain of the most authentic historians of those parts, who have been careful in collecting and collating the floating facts concerning this spectre, allege that the body of the trooper having been buried in the churchyard, the ghost rides forth to the scene of battle in nightly quest of his head, and that the rushing speed with which he sometimes passes along the Hollow, like a midnight blast, is owing to his being belated and in a hurry to get back to the churchyard before daybreak.

Such is the general purport of this legendary superstition, which has furnished materials for many a wild story in that region of shadows; and the spectre is known at all the country firesides by the name of the Headless Horseman of Sleepy Hollow.

It is remarkable that the visionary propensity I have mentioned is not confined to the native inhabitants of the valley, but is unconsciously imbibed by everyone who resides there for a time. However wide awake they may have been before they entered that sleepy region, they are sure in a little time to inhale the witching influence of the air and begin to grow imaginative—to dream dreams and see apparitions.

I mention this peaceful spot with all possible laud, for it is in such little, retired Dutch valleys, found here and there embosomed in the great State of New York, that population, manners, and customs remain fixed, while the great torrent of migration and improvement, which is making such incessant changes in other parts of this restless country, sweeps by them unobserved. They are like those little nooks of still water which border a rapid stream, where we may see the straw and bubble riding quietly at anchor or slowly revolving in their mimic harbor, undisturbed by the rush of the passing current. Though many years have elapsed since I trod the drowsy shades of Sleepy Hollow, yet I question whether I should not still find the same trees and the same families vegetating in its sheltered bosom.

In this by-place of Nature, there abode in a remote period of American history—that is to say, some thirty years since—a worthy wight of the name of Ichabod Crane, who sojourned, or, as he expressed it, "tarried," in Sleepy Hollow for the purpose of instructing the children of the vicinity. He was a native of Connecticut, a state which supplies the Union with pioneers for the mind as well as for the forest, and sends forth yearly its legions of frontier woodmen and country schoolmasters. The cognomen of Crane was not inapplicable to his person. He was tall, but exceedingly lank, with narrow shoulders, long arms and legs, hands that dangled a mile out of his sleeves, feet that might have served for shovels, and his whole frame most loosely hung together. His head was small, and flat at top, with huge ears, large, green, glassy eyes, and a long, snip nose, so that it looked like a weathercock perched upon his spindle neck to tell which way the wind blew. To see him striding along the profile of a hill on a windy day, with

*To see him striding along, one might have mistaken
him for the genius of famine*

his clothes bagging and fluttering about him, one might have mistaken him for the genius of famine descending upon the earth or some scarecrow eloped from a cornfield.

His schoolhouse was a low building of one large room, rudely constructed of logs, the windows partly glazed and partly patched with leaves of old copybooks. It was most ingeniously secured at vacant hours by a withe twisted in the handle of the door and stakes set against the window shutters, so that, though a thief might get in with perfect ease, he would find some embarrassment in getting out—an idea most probably borrowed by the architect, Yost Van Houten, from the mystery of an eelpot. The schoolhouse stood in a rather lonely but pleasant situation, just at the foot of a woody hill, with a brook running close by and a formidable birch tree growing at one end of it. From hence, the low murmur of his pupils' voices, conning over their lessons, might be heard in a drowsy summer's day like the hum of a beehive, interrupted now and then by the authoritative voice of the master in the tone of menace or command, or, peradventure, by the appalling sound of the birch as he urged some tardy loiterer along the flowery path of knowledge. Truth to say, he was a conscientious man, and ever bore in mind the golden maxim, "Spare the rod and spoil the child." Ichabod Crane's scholars certainly were not spoiled.

I would not have it imagined, however, that he

was one of those cruel potentates of the school
who joy in the smart of their subjects; on the
contrary, he administered justice with discrimi-
nation rather than severity, taking the burden off
the backs of the weak and laying it on those of the
strong. Your mere puny stripling, that winced at
the least flourish of the rod, was passed by with
indulgence; but the claims of justice were satisfied
by inflicting a double portion on some little,
tough, wrong-headed, broad-skirted Dutch urchin,
who sulked and swelled and grew dogged and
sullen beneath the birch. All this he called "doing his duty by their parents"; and he never inflicted a chastisement without following it by the
assurance, so consolatory to the smarting urchin,
that "he would remember it and thank him for it
the longest day he had to live."

When school hours were over, he was even the
companion and playmate of the larger boys, and
on holiday afternoons would convoy home some
of the smaller ones who happened to have pretty
sisters or good housewives for mothers noted for
the comforts of the cupboard. Indeed, it behooved
him to keep on good terms with his pupils. The
revenue arising from his school was small, and
would have been scarcely sufficient to furnish him
with daily bread, for he was a huge feeder, and,
though lank, had the dilating powers of an ana-
conda; but to help out his maintenance he was,
according to country custom in those parts,
boarded and lodged at the houses of the farmers

whose children he instructed. With these, he lived successively a week at a time, thus going the rounds of the neighborhood with all his worldly effects tied up in a cotton handkerchief.

That all this might not be too onerous on the purses of his rustic patrons, who were apt to consider the costs of schooling a grievous burden and schoolmasters as mere drones, he had various ways of rendering himself both useful and agreeable. He assisted the farmers occasionally in the lighter labors of their farms, helped to make hay, mended the fences, took the horses to water, drove the cows from pasture, and cut wood for the winter fire. He laid aside, too, all the dominant dignity and absolute sway with which he lorded it in his little empire, the school, and became wonderfully gentle and ingratiating. He found favor in the eyes of the mothers by petting the children, particularly the youngest; and like the lion bold, which whilom so magnanimously the lamb did hold, he would sit with a child on one knee and rock a cradle with his foot for whole hours together.

In addition to his other vocations, he was the singing master of the neighborhood and picked up many bright shillings by instructing the young folks in psalmody. It was a matter of no little vanity to him on Sundays to take his station in front of the church gallery with a band of chosen singers, where, in his own wind, he completely carried away the palm from the parson. Certain it is, his voice resounded far above all the rest of the congregation, and there are peculiar quavers still to be heard in that church, and which may even be heard half a mile off, quite to the opposite side of the millpond on a still Sunday morning, which are said to be legitimately descended from the nose of Ichabod Crane. Thus, by divers little makeshifts in the ingenious way which is commonly denominated "by hook and by crook," the worthy pedagogue got on tolerably enough, and was thought, by all who understood nothing of the labor of headwork, to have a wonderfully easy life of it.

The schoolmaster is generally a man of some importance in the female circle of a rural neighborhood, being considered a kind of idle, gentlemanlike personage of vastly superior taste and accomplishments to the rough country swains, and, indeed, inferior in learning only to the parson. His appearance, therefore, is apt to occasion some little stir at the tea table of a farmhouse and the addition of a supernumerary dish of cakes or sweetmeats, or, peradventure, the parade of a silver teapot. Our man of letters, therefore, was peculiarly happy in the smiles of all the country damsels. How he would figure among them in the churchyard between services on Sundays, gathering grapes for them from the wild vines that overrun the surrounding trees; reciting for their amusement all the epitaphs on the tombstones; or sauntering, with a whole bevy of them, along the banks of the adjacent millpond, while

the more bashful country bumpkins hung sheep-
ishly back, envying his superior elegance and
address.

From his half-itinerant life, also, he was a kind
of traveling gazette, carrying the whole budget
of local gossip from house to house, so that his
appearance was always greeted with satisfaction.
He was, moreover, esteemed by the women as a
man of great erudition, for he had read several
books quite through, and was a perfect master of
Cotton Mather's *History of New England Witchcraft*, in which, by the way, he most firmly and
potently believed.

He was, in fact, an odd mixture of small shrewdness and simple credulity. His appetite for the
marvelous and his powers of digesting it were
equally extraordinary, and both had been increased by his residence in this spellbound region.
No tale was too gross or monstrous for his capaci-
ous swallow. It was often his delight, after his
school was dismissed in the afternoon, to stretch
himself on the rich bed of clover bordering the
little brook that whimpered by his schoolhouse,
and there con over old Mather's direful tales until
the gathering dusk of the evening made the
printed page a mere mist before his eyes. Then,
as he wended his way by swamp and stream and
awful woodland to the farmhouse where he happened to be quartered, every sound of Nature at
that witching hour fluttered his excited imagination—the moan of the whip-poor-will from the

hillside; the boding cry of the tree toad, that harbinger of storm; the dreary hooting of the screech owl, or the sudden rustling in the thicket of birds frightened from their roost. The fireflies, too, which sparkled most vividly in the darkest places, now and then startled him as one of uncommon brightness would stream across his path; and if, by chance, a huge blockhead of a beetle came winging his blundering flight against him, the poor varlet was ready to give up the ghost, with the idea that he was struck with a witch's token. His only resource on such occasions, either to drown thought or drive away evil spirits, was to sing psalm tunes; and the good people of Sleepy Hollow, as they sat by their doors of an evening, were often filled with awe at hearing his nasal melody, "in linkèd sweetness long drawn out," floating from the distant hill or along the dusky road.

Another of his sources of fearful pleasure was to pass long winter evenings with the old Dutch wives as they sat spinning by the fire, with a row of apples roasting and spluttering along the hearth, and listen to their marvelous tales of ghosts and goblins, and haunted fields, and haunted brooks, and haunted bridges, and haunted houses, and particularly of the headless horseman, or Galloping Hessian of the Hollow, as they sometimes called him. He would delight them equally by his anecdotes of witchcraft and of the direful omens and portentous sights and sounds

in the air which prevailed in the earlier times of
Connecticut, and would frighten them woefully
with speculations upon comets and shooting stars,
and with the alarming fact that the world did absolutely turn round and that they were half the
time topsy-turvy.

But if there was a pleasure in all this while
snugly cuddling in the chimney corner of a
chamber that was all of a ruddy glow from the
crackling wood fire, and where, of course, no
spectre dared to show its face, it was dearly pur-
chased by the terrors of his subsequent walk homewards. What fearful shapes and shadows beset his
path amidst the dim and ghastly glare of a snowy
night! With what wistful look did he eye every
trembling ray of light streaming across the waste
fields from some distant window! How often was
he appalled by some shrub covered with snow,
which, like a sheeted spectre, beset his very path!
How often did he shrink with curdling awe at the
sound of his own steps on the frosty crust beneath
his feet, and dread to look over his shoulder,
lest he should behold some uncouth being tramp-
ing close behind him! And how often was he
thrown into complete dismay by some rushing
blast howling among the trees, in the idea that it
was the Galloping Hessian on one of his nightly
scourings!

All these, however, were mere terrors of the
night, phantoms of the mind that walk in darkness; and though he had seen many spectres in

She was a blooming lass of fresh eighteen

his time, and been more than once beset by Satan in divers shapes in his lonely perambulations, yet daylight put an end to all these evils; and he would have passed a pleasant life of it, in despite of the devil and all his works, if his path had not been crossed by a being that causes more perplexity to mortal man than ghosts, goblins, and the whole race of witches put together, and that was—a woman.

Among the musical disciples who assembled one evening in each week to receive his instructions in psalmody was Katrina Van Tassel, the daughter and only child of a substantial Dutch farmer. She was a blooming lass of fresh eighteen, plump as a partridge, ripe and melting and rosy-cheeked as one of her father's peaches, and universally famed, not merely for her beauty, but her vast expectations. She was withal a little of a coquette, as might be perceived even in her dress, which was a mixture of ancient and modern fashions, as most suited to set off her charms. She wore the ornaments of pure yellow gold which her great-great-grandmother had brought over from Saardam, the tempting stomacher of the olden time, and withal a provokingly short petticoat to display the prettiest foot and ankle in the country round.

Ichabod Crane had a soft and foolish heart towards the sex, and it is not to be wondered at that so tempting a morsel soon found favor in his eyes, more especially after he had visited her in her

paternal mansion. Old Baltus Van Tassel was a
perfect picture of a thriving, contented liberal-
hearted farmer. He seldom, it is true, sent either
his eyes or his thoughts beyond the boundaries of
his own farm, but within those everything was
snug, happy, and well conditioned. He was satisfied with his wealth, but not proud of it, and
piqued himself upon the hearty abundance,
rather than the style, in which he lived. His
stronghold was situated on the banks of the Hudson, in one of those green, sheltered, fertile nooks
in which the Dutch farmers are so fond of nest-
ling. A great elm tree spread its broad branches
over it, at the foot of which bubbled up a spring
of the softest and sweetest water in a little well,
formed of a barrel, and then stole sparkling away
through the grass to a neighboring brook that bubbled along among alders and dwarf willows. Hard
by the farmhouse was a vast barn, that might have
served for a church, every window and crevice of
which seemed bursting forth with the treasures of
the farm; the flail was busily resounding within it
from morning to night; swallows and martins
skimmed twittering about the eaves; and rows of
pigeons, some with one eye turned up, as if watching the weather, some with their heads under their
wings or buried in their bosoms, and others, swelling, and cooing, and bowing about their dames,
were enjoying the sunshine on the roof. Sleek, un-
wieldy porkers were grunting in the repose and
abundance of their pens, whence sallied forth,

now and then, troops of sucking pigs as if to sniff the air. A stately squadron of snowy geese were riding in an adjoining pond, convoying whole fleets of ducks; regiments of turkeys were gobbling through the farmyard, and guinea-fowls fretting about it, like ill-tempered housewives, with their peevish, discontented cry. Before the barn door strutted the gallant cock, that pattern of a husband, a warrior, and a fine gentleman, clapping his burnished wings and crowing in the pride and gladness of his heart—sometimes tearing up the earth with his feet, and then generously calling his ever-hungry family of wives and children to enjoy the rich morsel which he had discovered.

The pedagogue's mouth watered as he looked upon this sumptuous promise of luxurious winter fare. In his devouring mind's eye he pictured to himself every roasting-pig running about with a pudding in his belly and an apple in his mouth; the pigeons were snugly put to bed in a comfortable pie and tucked in with a coverlet of crust; the geese were swimming in their own gravy; and the ducks pairing cosily in dishes, like snug married couples, with a decent competency of onion sauce. In the porkers he saw carved out the future sleek side of bacon and juicy relishing ham; not a turkey but he beheld daintily trussed up, with its gizzard under its wing, and, peradventure, a necklace of savory sausages; and even bright Chanticleer himself lay sprawling on his back in a side dish, with uplifted claws, as if craving that quarter which his chivalrous spirit disdained to ask while living.

As the enraptured Ichabod fancied all this, and as he rolled his great green eyes over the fat meadowlands, the rich fields of wheat, of rye, of buckwheat, and Indian corn, and the orchards burdened with ruddy fruit, which surrounded the warm tenement of Van Tassel, his heart yearned after the damsel who was to inherit these domains, and his imagination expanded with the idea how they might be readily turned into cash and the money invested in immense tracts of wild land and shingle palaces in the wilderness. Nay, his busy fancy already realized his hopes, and presented to him the blooming Katrina, with a whole family of children, mounted on the top of a wagon loaded with household trumpery, with pots and kettles dangling beneath, and he beheld himself bestriding a pacing mare, with a colt at her heels, setting out for Kentucky, Tennessee, or the Lord knows where.

When he entered the house the conquest of his heart was complete. It was one of those spacious farmhouses, with high-ridged but low-sloping roofs, built in the style handed down from the first Dutch settlers, the low projecting eaves forming a piazza along the front capable of being closed up in bad weather. Under this were hung flails, harness, various utensils of husbandry, and nets for fishing in the neighborhood river. Benches were built along the sides for summer use, and a

great spinning-wheel at one end and a churn at
the other showed the various uses to which this
important porch might be devoted. From this
piazza the wondering Ichabod entered the hall,
which formed the center of the mansion and the
place of usual residence. Here rows of resplendent
pewter, ranged on a long dresser, dazzled his eyes.
In one corner stood a huge bag of wool ready to
be spun; in another a quantity of linsey-woolsey
just from the loom; ears of Indian corn and strings
of dried apples and peaches hung in gay festoon
along the walls, mingled with the gaud of red
peppers; and a door left ajar gave him a peep into
the best parlor, where the claw-footed chairs and
dark mahogany tables shone like mirrors; andirons,
with their accompanying shovel and tongs,
glistened from their covert of asparagus tops;
mock-oranges and conch-shells decorated the
mantelpiece; strings of various-colored birds' eggs
were suspended above it; a great ostrich egg was
hung from the center of the room, and a corner
cupboard, knowingly left open, displayed immense treasures of old silver and well-mended
china.

From the moment Ichabod laid his eyes upon
these regions of delight the peace of his mind was
at an end, and his only study was how to gain the
affections of the peerless daughter of Van Tassel.
In this enterprise, however, he had more real difficulties than generally fell to the lot of a knight-
errant of yore, who seldom had anything but

giants, enchanters, fiery dragons, and such-like easily conquered adversaries to contend with, and had to make his way merely through gates of iron and brass and walls of adamant to the castle keep, where the lady of his heart was confined; all of which he achieved as easily as a man would carve his way to the center of a Christmas pie, and then the lady gave him her hand as a matter of course. Ichabod, on the contrary, had to win his way to the heart of a country coquette beset with a labyrinth of whims and caprices, which were forever presenting new difficulties and impediments, and he had to encounter a host of fearful adversaries of real flesh and blood, the numerous rustic admirers who beset every portal to her heart, keeping a watchful and angry eye upon each other, but ready to fly out in the common cause against any new competitor.

Among these the most formidable was a burly, roaring, roistering blade of the name of Abraham —or, according to the Dutch abbreviation, Brom —Van Brunt, the hero of the country round, which rang with his feats of strength and hardihood. He was broad-shouldered and double-jointed, with short curly black hair and a bluff but not unpleasant countenance, having a mingled air of fun and arrogance. From his Herculean frame and great powers of limb, he had received the nickname of "Brom Bones," by which he was universally known. He was famed for great knowledge and skill in horsemanship, being as dextrous on horseback as a Tartar. He was foremost at all races and cockfights, and, with the ascendency which bodily strength acquires in rustic life, was the umpire in all disputes, setting his hat on one side and giving his decisions with an air and tone admitting of no gainsay or appeal. He was always ready for either a fight or a frolic, but had more mischief than ill-will in his composition; and with all his overbearing roughness there was a strong dash of waggish good humor at bottom. He had three or four boon companions, who regarded him as their model, and at the head of whom he scoured the country, attending every scene of feud or merriment for miles around. In cold weather he was distinguished by a fur cap surmounted with a flaunting fox's tail; and when folks at a country gathering descried this well-known crest at a distance, whisking about among a squad of hard riders, they always stood by for a squall. Sometimes his crew would be heard dashing along past the farmhouses at midnight with whoop and halloo, like a troop of Don Cossacks, and the old dames, startled out of their sleep, would listen for a moment till the hurry-scurry had clattered by, and then exclaim, "Ay, there goes Brom Bones and his gang!" The neighbors looked upon him with a mixture of awe, admiration, and good will, and when any madcap prank or rustic brawl occurred in the vicinity, always shook their heads and warranted Brom Bones was at the bottom of it.

This rantipole hero had for some time singled out the blooming Katrina for the object of his uncouth gallantries, and, though his amorous toyings were something like the gentle caresses and endearments of a bear, yet it was whispered that she did not altogether discourage his hopes. Certain it is, his advances were signals for rival candidates to retire who felt no inclination to cross a line in his amours; insomuch, that when his horse was seen tied to Van Tassel's paling on a Sunday night, a sure sign that his master was courting—or, as it is termed "sparking"—within, all other suitors passed by in despair and carried the war into other quarters.

Such was the formidable rival with whom Ichabod Crane had to contend, and, considering all things, a stouter man than he would have shrunk from the competition and a wiser man would have despaired. He had, however, a happy mixture of pliability and perseverance in his nature; he was in form and spirit like a supple jack—yielding, but tough; though he bent, he never broke; and though he bowed beneath the slightest pressure, yet the moment it was away, jerk! He was as erect and carried his head as high as ever.

To have taken the field openly against his rival would have been madness; for he was not a man to be thwarted in his amours, any more than that stormy lover, Achilles. Ichabod, therefore, made his advances in a quiet and gently insinuating manner. Under cover of his character of singing master he made frequent visits at the farmhouse; not that he had anything to apprehend from the meddlesome interference of parents, which is so often a stumbling-block in the path of lovers. Balt Van Tassel was an easy, indulgent soul; he loved his daughter better even than his pipe, and, like a reasonable man and an excellent father, let her have her way in everything. His notable little wife, too, had enough to do to attend to her house-keeping and manage her poultry; for, as she sagely observed, ducks and geese are foolish things and must be looked after, but girls can take care of themselves. Thus while the busy dame bustled about the house or plied her spinning-wheel at one end of the piazza, honest Balt would sit smoking his evening pipe at the other, watching the achievements of a little wooden warrior who, armed with a sword in each hand, was most val-iantly fighting the wind on the pinnacle of the barn. In the meantime, Ichabod would carry on his suit with the daughter by the side of the spring under the great elm or sauntering along in the twilight, that hour so favorable to the lover's eloquence. I profess not to know how women's hearts are wooed and won. To me they have al-ways been matters of riddle and admiration. Some seem to have but one vulnerable point or door of access, while others have a thousand avenues and may be captured in a thousand different ways. It is a great triumph of skill to gain the former, but a still greater proof of generalship to maintain possession of the latter, for a man must battle for his fortress at every door and window. He who wins a thousand common hearts is therefore entitled to some renown, but he who keeps undisputed sway over the heart of a coquette is indeed a hero. Certain it is, this was not the case with the redoubtable Brom Bones; and from the moment Ichabod Crane made his advances, the interests of the former evidently declined, his horse was no longer seen tied at the palings on Sunday nights, and a deadly feud gradually arose between him and the preceptor of Sleepy Hollow.

Brom, who had a degree of rough chivalry in his nature, would fain have carried matters to open warfare, and have settled their pretensions to the lady according to the mode of those most concise and simple reasoners, the knights-errant of yore—by single combat; but Ichabod was too conscious of the superior might of his adversary to enter the lists against him. He had overheard a boast of Bones, that he would "double the schoolmaster up and lay him on a shelf of his own schoolhouse;" and he was too wary to give him an opportunity. There was something extremely provoking in this obstinately pacific system; it left Brom no alternative but to draw upon the funds of rustic waggery in his disposition and to play off boorish practical jokes upon his rival. Ichabod became the object of whimsical persecution to Bones and his gang of rough riders. They harried his hitherto peaceful domains; smoked out his singing school by stopping up the chimney; broke into the schoolhouse at night, in spite of its formidable fastenings of withe and window stakes, and turned everything topsy-turvy; so that the poor schoolmaster began to think all the witches in the country held their meetings there. But, what was still more annoying, Brom took all opportunities of turning him into ridicule in the presence of his mistress, and had a scoundrel dog whom he taught to whine in the most ludicrous manner, and introduced as a rival of Ichabod's to instruct her in psalmody.

In this way matters went on for some time without producing any material effect on the relative situation of the contending powers. On a fine autumnal afternoon Ichabod, in pensive mood, sat enthroned on the lofty stool whence he usually watched all the concerns of his little literary realm. In his hand he swayed a ferule, that sceptre of despotic power; the birch of justice reposed on three nails behind the throne, a constant terror to evildoers; while on the desk before him might be seen sundry contraband articles and prohibited weapons detected upon the persons of idle urchins, such as half-munched apples, popguns, whirligigs, fly-cages, and whole legions of rampant little paper gamecocks. Apparently there had been some appalling act of justice recently inflicted, for his scholars were all busily intent upon their books or slyly whispering behind them with one eye kept upon the master, and a kind of buzzing stillness reigned throughout the schoolroom. It was suddenly interrupted by the appearance of a Negro in tow-cloth jacket and trousers, a round-crowned fragment of a hat like the cap of Mercury, and mounted on the back of a ragged, wild, half-broken colt, which he managed with a rope by way of halter. He came clattering up to the school door with an invitation to Ichabod to attend a merrymaking or "quilting frolic" to be held that evening at Mynheer Van Tassel's; and, having delivered his message, he dashed over the brook, and was seen scampering away up the hollow, full of the importance and hurry of his mission.

All was now bustle and hubbub in the late quiet schoolroom. The scholars were hurried through their lessons without stopping at trifles; those who were nimble skipped over half with impunity, and those who were tardy had a smart application now and then in the rear to quicken their speed or help them over a tall word. Books were flung aside without being put away on the shelves, inkstands were overturned, benches thrown down, and the whole school was turned loose an hour before the usual time, bursting forth like a legion of young imps, yelping and racketing about the green in joy at their early emancipation.

The gallant Ichabod now spent at least an extra half hour at his toilet, brushing and furbishing up his best, and indeed only, suit of rusty black and arranging his locks by a bit of broken looking glass that hung up in the schoolhouse. That he might make his appearance before his mistress in the true style of a cavalier, he borrowed a horse from the farmer with whom he was domiciliated, a choleric old Dutchman of the name of Hans Van Ripper, and, thus gallantly mounted, issued forth like a knight-errant in quest of adventures. But it is meet I should, in the true spirit of romantic story, give some account of the looks and equipments of my hero and his steed. The animal he bestrode was a broken-down plowhorse that had outlived almost everything but his viciousness. He was gaunt and shagged, with a ewe neck and a head like a hammer; his rusty mane and tail were tangled and knotted with burrs; one eye had lost its pupil and was glaring and spectral, but the other had the gleam of a genuine devil in it. Still, he must have had fire and mettle in his day, if we may judge from the name he bore of Gunpowder. He had, in fact, been a favorite steed of his master, the choleric Van Ripper, who was a furious rider, and had infused, very probably, some of his own spirit into the animal; for, old and broken down as he looked, there was more of the lurking devil in him than in any young filly in the country.

Ichabod was a suitable figure for such a steed. He rode with short stirrups, which brought his knees nearly up to the pommel of the saddle; his sharp elbows stuck out like a grasshopper's; he carried his whip perpendicularly in his hand like a sceptre; and as his horse jogged on, the motion of his arms was not unlike the flapping of a pair of wings. A small wool hat rested on the top of his nose, for so his scanty strip of forehead might be called, and the skirts of his black coat fluttered out almost to his horse's tail. Such was the appearance of Ichabod and his steed as they shambled out of the gate of Hans Van Ripper, and it was altogether such an apparition as is seldom to be met with in broad daylight.

It was, as I have said, a fine autumnal day, the sky was clear and serene, and Nature wore that rich and golden livery which we always associate with the idea of abundance. The forests had put on their sober brown and yellow, while some trees of the tender kind had been nipped by the frosts into brilliant dyes of orange, purple, and scarlet. Streaming files of wild ducks began to make their appearance high in the air; the bark of the squirrel might be heard from the groves of beech and hickory nuts, and the pensive whistle of the quail at intervals from the neighboring stubble field.

The small birds were taking their farewell banquets. In the fullness of their revelry they fluttered, chirping and frolicking, from bush to bush and tree to tree, capricious from the very profusion and variety around them. There was the honest cock robin, the favorite game of stripling sportsmen, with its loud querulous note; and the twittering blackbirds, flying in sable clouds; and the golden-winged woodpecker, with his crimson crest, his broad black gorget, and splendid plumages, and the cedar-bird, with its red-tipped wings and yellow-tipped tail, and its little monteiro cap of feathers; and the blue jay, that noisy coxcomb, in his gay light-blue coat and white underclothes, screaming and chattering, bobbing and nodding and bowing, and pretending to be on good terms with every songster of the grove.

As Ichabod jogged slowly on his way his eye, ever open to every symptom of culinary abundance, ranged with delight over the treasures of jolly Autumn. On all sides he beheld vast store of apples—some hanging in oppressive opulence on the trees, some gathered into baskets and barrels for the market, others heaped up in rich piles for the cider press. Farther on he beheld great fields of Indian corn, with its golden ears peeping from their leafy coverts and holding out the promise of cakes and hasty pudding; and the yellow pumpkins lying beneath them, turning up their fair round bellies to the sun, and giving ample prospects of the most luxurious of pies; and anon he passed the fragrant buckwheat fields, breathing the odor of the beehive, and as he beheld them soft anticipations stole over his mind of dainty slapjacks, well buttered and garnished with honey or treacle by the delicate little dimpled hand of Katrina Van Tassel.

Thus, feeding his mind with many sweet thoughts and "sugared suppositions," he journeyed along the sides of a range of hills which look out upon some of the goodliest scenes of the mighty Hudson. The sun gradually wheeled his broad disk down into the west. The wide bosom of the Tappan Zee lay motionless and glassy, excepting that here and there a gentle undulation waved and prolonged the blue shadow of the distant mountain. A few amber clouds floated in the sky, without a breath of air to move them. The horizon was of a fine golden tint, changing gradually into a pure apple green, and from that into the deep blue of the mid-heaven. A slanting ray lingered on the woody crests of the precipices that overhung some parts of the river, giving greater depth to the dark gray and purple of their rocky sides. A sloop was loitering in the distance, dropping slowly down with the tide, her sail hanging uselessly against the mast, and, as the reflection of the sky gleamed along the still water it seemed as if the vessel was suspended in the air.

It was toward evening that Ichabod arrived at the castle of the Heer Van Tassel, which he found thronged with the pride and flower of the adjacent country—old farmers, a spare, leathern-faced race, in homespun coats and breeches, blue stockings, huge shoes, and magnificent pewter buckles; their brisk withered little dames, in close crimped caps, long-waisted short-gowns, homespun petticoats, with scissors and pincushions and gay calico pockets hanging on the outside; buxom lassies, almost as antiquated as their mothers, excepting where a straw hat, a fine ribbon, or perhaps a white frock, gave symptoms of city innovation; the sons, in short square-skirted coats with rows of stupendous brass buttons, and their hair generally queued in the fashion of the times, especially if they could procure an eel-skin for the purpose, it being esteemed throughout the country as a potent nourisher and strengthener of the hair.

Brom Bones, however, was the hero of the scene, having come to the gathering on his favorite steed Daredevil—a creature, like himself, full of metal and mischief, and which no one but himself could manage. He was, in fact, noted for preferring vicious animals, given to all kinds of tricks, which kept the rider in constant risk of his neck, for he held a tractable, well-broken horse as unworthy of a lad of spirit.

Fain would I pause to dwell upon the world of charms that burst upon the enraptured gaze of my hero as he entered the state parlor of Van Tassel's mansion. Not those of the bevy of buxom lasses with their luxurious display of red and white, but the ample charms of a genuine Dutch country tea table in the sumptuous time of autumn. Such heaped-up platters of cakes of various and almost indescribable kinds, known only to experienced Dutch housewives! There was the doughty doughnut, the tenderer oily koek, and the crisp and crumbling cruller; sweet cakes and shortcakes, ginger cakes and honey cakes, and the whole family of cakes. And then there were apple pies and peach pies and pumpkin pies; besides slices of ham and smoked beef; and moreover, delectable

dishes of preserved plums and peaches and pears
and quinces; not to mention broiled shad and
roasted chicken; together with bowls of milk and
cream—all mingled higgledy-piggledy, pretty
much as I have enumerated them, with the
motherly teapot sending up its clouds of vapor
from the midst. Heaven bless the mark! I want
breath and time to discuss this banquet as it de-
serves, and am too eager to get on with my story.
Happily, Ichabod Crane was not in so great a
hurry as his historian, but did ample justice to
every dainty.

He was a kind and thankful creature, whose
heart dilated in proportion as his skin was filled
with good cheer, and whose spirits rose with eat-
ing as some men's do with drink. He could not
help, too, rolling his large eyes round him as he
ate, and chuckling with the possibility that he
might one day be lord of all this scene of almost
unimaginable luxury and splendor. Then, he
thought, how soon he'd turn his back upon the
old schoolhouse, snap his fingers in the face of
Hans Van Ripper and every other niggardly
patron, and kick any itinerant pedagogue out of
doors that should dare to call him comrade!

Old Baltus Van Tassel moved about among his
guests with a face dilated with content and good
humor, round and jolly as the harvest moon. His
hospitable attentions were brief, but expressive,
being confined to a shake of the hand, a slap on
the shoulder, a loud laugh, and a pressing invitation to "fall to and help themselves."

And now the sound of the music from the common room, or hall, summoned to the dance. The musician was an old gray-headed Negro who had been the itinerant orchestra of the neighborhood for more than half a century. His instrument was as old and battered as himself. The greater part of the time he scraped on two or three strings, accompanying every movement of the bow with a motion of the head, bowing almost to the ground and stamping with his foot whenever a fresh couple were to start.

Ichabod prided himself upon his dancing as much as upon his vocal powers. Not a limb, not a fibre about him was idle; and to have seen his loosely hung frame in full motion and clattering about the room you would have thought Saint Vitus himself, that blessed patron of the dance, was figuring before you in person. He was the admiration of all the Negroes, who, having gathered, of all ages and sizes, from the farm and the neighborhood, stood forming a pyramid of shining black faces at every door and window, gazing with delight at the scene, rolling their white eyeballs, and showing grinning rows of ivory from ear to ear. How could the flogger of urchins be otherwise than animated and joyous? The lady of his heart was his partner in the dance, and smiling graciously in reply to all his amorous oglings, while Brom Bones, sorely smitten with love and jealousy, sat brooding by himself in one corner.

When the dance was at an end Ichabod was attracted to a knot of the sager folks, who, with old Van Tassel, sat smoking at one end of the piazza gossiping over former times and drawing out long stories about the war.

This neighborhood, at the time of which I am speaking, was one of those highly favored places which abound with chronicle and great men. The British and American line had run near it during the war; it had therefore been the scene of marauding and infested with refugees, cowboys, and all kinds of border chivalry. Just sufficient time had elapsed to enable each storyteller to dress up his tale with a little becoming fiction, and in the indistinctness of his recollection to make himself the hero of every exploit.

There was the story of Doffue Martling, a large blue-bearded Dutchman, who had nearly taken a British frigate with an old iron nine-pounder from a mud breastwork, only that his gun burst at the sixth discharge. And there was an old gentleman who shall be nameless, being too rich a mynheer to be lightly mentioned, who, in the battle of Whiteplains, being an excellent master of defense, parried a musket-ball with a small sword, insomuch that he absolutely felt it whiz round the blade and glance off at the hilt: in proof of which he was ready at any time to show the sword, with the hilt a little bent. There were several more that had been equally great in the field, not one of whom but was persuaded that he had a considerable hand in bringing the war to a happy termination.

But all these were nothing to the tales of ghosts and apparitions that succeeded. The neighborhood is rich in legendary treasures of the kind. Local tales and superstitions thrive best in these sheltered, long-settled retreats, but are trampled underfoot by the shifting throng that forms the population of most of our country places. Besides, there is no encouragement for ghosts in most of our villages, for they have scarcely had time to finish their first nap and turn themselves in their graves before their surviving friends have traveled away from the neighborhood; so that when they turn out at night to walk their rounds they have no acquaintance left to call upon. This is perhaps the reason why we so seldom hear of ghosts except in our long-established Dutch communities.

The immediate cause, however, of the prevalence of supernatural stories in these parts was doubtless owing to the vicinity of Sleepy Hollow. There was a contagion in the very air that blew from that haunted region; it breathed forth an atmosphere of dreams and fancies infecting all the land. Several of the Sleepy Hollow people were present at Van Tassel's, and, as usual, were doling out their wild and wonderful legends. Many dismal tales were told about funeral trains and mourning cries and wailings heard and seen about the great tree where the unfortunate Major André was taken, and which stood in the neighborhood. Some mention was made also of the woman in white that haunted the dark glen at Raven

Rock, and was often heard to shriek on winter nights before a storm, having perished there in the snow. The chief part of the stories, however, turned upon the favorite spectre of Sleepy Hollow, the headless horseman, who had been heard several times of late patroling the country, and, it was said, tethered his horse nightly among the graves in the churchyard.

The sequestered situation of this church seems always to have made it a favorite haunt of troubled spirits. It stands on a knoll surrounded by locust trees and lofty elms, from among which its decent whitewashed walls shine modestly forth, like Christian purity beaming through the shades of retirement. A gentle slope descends from it to a silver sheet of water bordered by high trees, between which peeps may be caught at the blue hills of the Hudson. To look upon its grass-grown yard, where the sunbeams seem to sleep so quietly, one would think that there at least the dead might rest in peace. On one side of the church extends a wide woody dell, along which raves a large brook among broken rocks and trunks of fallen trees. Over a deep black part of the stream, not far from the church, was formerly thrown a wooden bridge; the road that led to it and the bridge itself were thickly shaded by overhanging trees, which cast a gloom about it even in the daytime, but occasioned a fearful darkness at night. Such was one of the favorite haunts of the headless horseman, and the place where he was most frequently encountered. The tale was told of old Brouwer, a most heretical disbeliever in ghosts, how he met the horseman returning from his foray into Sleepy Hollow, and was obliged to get up behind him; how they galloped over bush and brake, over hill and swamp, until they reached the bridge, when the horseman suddenly turned into a skeleton, threw old Brouwer into the brook, and sprang away over the treetops with a clap of thunder.

This story was immediately matched by a thrice-marvelous adventure of Brom Bones, who made light of the galloping Hessian as an arrant jockey. He affirmed that on returning one night from the neighboring village of Sing-Sing he had been overtaken by this midnight trooper; that he had offered to race with him for a bowl of punch, and should have won it too, for Daredevil beat the goblin horse all hollow, but just as they came to the church bridge the Hessian bolted and vanished in a flash of fire.

All these tales, told in that drowsy undertone with which men talk in the dark, the countenances of the listeners only now and then receiving a casual gleam from the glare of a pipe, sank deep in the mind of Ichabod. He repaid them in kind with large extracts from his invaluable author, Cotton Mather, and added many marvelous events that had taken place in his native state of Connecticut and fearful sights which he had seen in his nightly walks about Sleepy Hollow.

The revel now gradually broke up. The old farmers gathered together their families in their wagons, and were heard for some time rattling along the hollow roads and over the distant hills. Some of the damsels mounted on pillions behind their favorite swains, and their lighthearted laughter, mingling with the clatter of hoofs, echoed along the silent woodlands, sounding fainter until they gradually died away, and the late scene of noise and frolic was all silent and deserted. Ichabod only lingered behind, according to the custom of country lovers, to have a tête-à-tête with the heiress, fully convinced that he was now on the highroad to success. What passed at this interview I will not pretend to say, for in fact I do not know. Something, however, I fear me, must have gone wrong, for he certainly sallied forth, after no very great interval, with an air quite desolate and chop-fallen. Oh, these women! These women! Could that girl have been playing off any of her coquettish tricks? Was her encouragement of the poor pedagogue all a mere sham to secure her conquest of his rival? Heaven only knows, not I! Let it suffice to say, Ichabod stole forth with the air of one who has been sacking a hen roost, rather than a fair lady's heart. Without looking to the right or left to notice the scene of rural wealth on which he had so often gloated, he went straight to the stable, and with several hearty cuffs and kicks roused his steed most uncourteously from the comfortable quarters in which he was soundly sleeping, dreaming of mountains of corn and oats and whole valleys of timothy and clover.

It was the very witching time of night that Ichabod, heavyhearted and crestfallen, pursued his travel homewards along the sides of the lofty hills which rise above Tarry Town, and which he had traversed so cheerily in the afternoon. The hour was as dismal as himself. Far below him the Tappan Zee spread its dusky and indistinct waste of waters, with here and there the tall mast of a sloop riding quietly at anchor under the land. In the dead hush of midnight he could even hear the barking of the watchdog from the opposite shore of the Hudson; but it was so vague and faint as only to give an idea of his distance from this faithful companion of man. Now and then, too, the long-drawn crowing of a cock, accidentally awakened, would sound far, far off, from some farmhouse away among the hills; but it was like a dreaming sound in his ear. No signs of life occurred near him, but occasionally the melancholy chirp of a cricket, or perhaps the guttural twang of a bullfrog from a neighboring marsh, as if sleeping uncomfortably and turning suddenly in his bed.

All the stories of ghosts and goblins that he had heard in the afternoon now came crowding upon his recollection. The night grew darker and darker; the stars seemed to sink deeper in the sky, and driving clouds occasionally hid them from his sight. He had never felt so lonely and dismal. He was, moreover, approaching the very place where many of the scenes of the ghost stories had been laid. In the center of the road stood an enormous tulip tree which towered like a giant above all the other trees of the neighborhood and formed a kind of landmark. Its limbs were gnarled and fantastic, large enough to form trunks for ordinary trees, twisting down almost to the earth and rising again into the air. It was connected with the tragical story of the unfortunate André, who had been taken prisoner hard by, and was universally known by the name of Major André's tree. The common people regarded it with a mixture of respect and superstition, partly out of sympathy for the fate of its ill-starred namesake, and partly from the tales of strange sights and doleful lamentations told concerning it.

As Ichabod approached this fearful tree he began to whistle: he thought his whistle was answered; it was but a blast sweeping sharply through the dry branches. As he approached a little nearer he thought he saw something white hanging in the midst of the tree: he paused and ceased whistling, but on looking more narrowly perceived that it was a place where the tree had been scathed by lightning and the white wood laid bare. Suddenly he heard a groan: his teeth chattered and his knees smote against the saddle; it was but the rubbing of one huge bough upon another as they were swayed about by the breeze.

He passed the tree in safety, but new perils lay before him.

About two hundred yards from the tree a small brook crossed the road and ran into a marshy and thickly wooded glen known by the name of Wiley's Swamp. A few rough logs, laid side by side, served for a bridge over the stream. On that side of the road where the brook entered the wood a group of oaks and chestnuts, matted thick with wild grapevines, threw a cavernous gloom over it. To pass this bridge was the severest trial. It was at this identical spot that the unfortunate André was captured, and under the covert of those chestnuts and vines were the sturdy yeomen concealed who surprised him. This has ever since been considered a haunted stream, and fearful are the feelings of the schoolboy who has to pass it alone after dark.

As he approached the stream his heart began to thump; he summoned up, however, all his resolution, gave his horse half a score of kicks in the ribs, and attempted to dash briskly across the bridge; but instead of starting forward, the perverse old animal made a lateral movement and ran broadside against the fence. Ichabod, whose fears increased with the delay, jerked the reins on the other side and kicked lustily with the contrary foot: it was all in vain; his steed started, it is true, but it was only to plunge to the opposite side of the road into a thicket of brambles and alder bushes. The schoolmaster now bestowed both whip and heel upon the starveling ribs of old Gunpowder, who dashed forward, snuffling and snorting, but came to a stand just by the bridge with a suddenness that had nearly sent his rider sprawling over his head. Just at this moment a plashy tramp by the side of the bridge caught the sensitive ear of Ichabod. In the dark shadow of the grove on the margin of the brook he beheld something huge, misshapen, black, and towering. It stirred not, but seemed gathered up into the gloom, like some gigantic monster ready to spring upon the traveler.

The hair of the affrighted pedagogue rose upon his head with terror. What was to be done? To turn and fly was now too late; and besides, what chance was there of escaping ghost or goblin, if such it was, which could ride upon the wings of the wind? Summoning up, therefore, a show of courage, he demanded in stammering accents, "Who are you?" He received no reply. He repeated his demand in a still more agitated voice. Still there was no answer. Once more he cudgeled the sides of the inflexible Gunpowder, and, shutting his eyes, broke forth with involuntary fervor into a psalm tune. Just then the shadowy object of alarm put itself in motion, and with a scramble and a bound stood at once in the middle of the road. Though the night was dark and dismal, yet the form of the unknown might now in some degree be ascertained. He appeared to be a horseman of large dimensions and mounted on a black horse of powerful frame. He made no offer of molestation or sociability, but kept aloof on one side of the road, jogging along on the blind side of old Gunpowder, who had now got over his fright and waywardness.

Ichabod, who had no relish for this strange midnight companion, and bethought himself of the adventure of Brom Bones with the Galloping Hessian, now quickened his steed in hopes of leaving him behind. The stranger, however, quickened his horse to an equal pace. Ichabod pulled up, and fell into a walk, thinking to lag behind; the other did the same. He heart began to sink within him; he endeavored to resume his psalm tune, but his parched tongue clove to the roof of his mouth and he could not utter a stave. There was something in the moody and dogged silence of this pertinacious companion that was mysterious and appalling. It was soon fearfully accounted for. On mounting a rising ground, which brought the figure of his fellow traveler in relief against the sky, gigantic in height and muffled in a cloak, Ichabod was horror-struck on perceiving that he was headless! But his horror was still more increased on observing that the head, which should have rested on his shoulders, was carried before him on the pommel of the saddle. His terror rose to desperation, he rained a shower of kicks and blows upon Gunpowder, hoping by a sudden movement to give his companion the slip; but the spectre started full jump with him. Away, then, they dashed through thick and thin, stones flying and sparks flashing at every bound. Ichabod's flimsy garments fluttered in the air as he stretched his long lank body away over his horse's head in the eagerness of his flight.

They had now reached the road which turns off to Sleepy Hollow; but Gunpowder, who seemed possessed with a demon, instead of keeping up it, made an opposite turn and plunged headlong downhill to the left. This road leads through a sandy hollow shaded by trees for about a quarter of a mile, where it crosses the bridge famous in goblin story, and just beyond swells the green knoll on which stands the whitewashed church.

As yet the panic of the steed had given his unskillful rider an apparent advantage in the chase; but just as he had got halfway through the hollow the girths of the saddle gave away and he felt it slipping from under him. He seized it by the pommel and endeavored to hold it firm, but in vain, and had just time to save himself by clasping old Gunpowder round the neck, when the saddle fell to the earth, and he heard it trampled underfoot by his pursuer. For a moment the terror of Hans Van Ripper's wrath passed across his mind, for it was his Sunday saddle; but this was no time for petty fears; the goblin was hard on his haunches, and (unskilled rider that he was) he had much ado to maintain his seat, sometimes slipping on one side, sometimes on another, and

Richard John

Spreading the News

Simmons

sometimes jolted on the high ridge of his horse's backbone with a violence that he verily feared would cleave him asunder.

An opening in the trees now cheered him with the hopes that the church bridge was at hand. The wavering reflection of a silver star in the bosom of the brook told him that he was not mistaken. He saw the walls of the church dimly glaring under the trees beyond. He recollected the place where Brom Bones' ghostly competitor had disappeared. "If I can but reach that bridge," thought Ichabod, "I am safe." Just then he heard the black steed panting and blowing close behind him; he even fancied that he felt his hot breath. Another convulsive kick in the ribs, and old Gunpowder sprang upon the bridge; he thundered over the resounding planks; he gained the opposite side; and now Ichabod cast a look behind to see if his pursuer should vanish, according to rule, in a flash of fire and brimstone. Just then he saw the goblin rising in his stirrups, and in the very act of hurling his head at him. Ichabod endeavored to dodge the horrible missile, but too late. It encountered his cranium with a tremendous crash; he was tumbled headlong into the dust, and Gunpowder, the black steed, and the goblin rider passed by like a whirlwind.

The next morning the old horse was found, without his saddle and with the bridle under his feet, soberly cropping the grass at his master's gate. Ichabod did not make his appearance at

Just then he saw the goblin rising in his stirrups

breakfast; dinner hour came, but no Ichabod. The boys assembled at the schoolhouse and strolled idly about the banks of the brook; but no schoolmaster. Hans Van Ripper now began to feel some uneasiness about the fate of poor Ichabod and his saddle. An inquiry was set on foot, and after diligent investigation they came upon his traces. In one part of the road leading to the church was found the saddle trampled in the dirt; the tracks of horses' hoofs, deeply dented in the road and evidently at furious speed, were traced to the bridge, beyond which, on the bank of a broad part of the brook, where the water ran deep and black, was found the hat of the unfortunate Ichabod, and close beside it a shattered pumpkin.

The brook was searched, but the body of the schoolmaster was not to be discovered. Hans Van Ripper, as executor of his estate, examined the bundle which contained all his worldly effects. They consisted of two shirts and a half, two stocks for the neck, a pair or two of worsted stockings, an old pair of corduroy small-clothes, a rusty razor, a book of psalm tunes full of dog's ears, and a broken pitchpipe. As to the books and furniture of the schoolhouse, they belonged to the community, excepting Cotton Mather's *History of Witchcraft*, a *New England Almanac*, and a book of dreams and fortune-telling; in which last was a sheet of foolscap much scribbled and blotted in several fruitless attempts to make a copy of verses in honor of the heiress of Van Tassel. These magic

books and the poetic scrawl were forthwith con-
signed to the flames by Hans Van Ripper, who
from that time forward determined to send his
children no more to school, observing that he
never knew any good come of this same reading
and writing. Whatever money the schoolmaster
possessed—and he had received his quarter's pay
but a day or two before—he must have had about
his person at the time of his disappearance.

The mysterious event caused much speculation
at the church on the following Sunday. Knots of
gazers and gossips were collected in the churchyard, at the bridge, and at the spot where the hat
and pumpkin had been found. The stories of
Brouwer, of Bones, and a whole budget of others
were called to mind, and when they had diligently
considered them all, and compared them with the
symptoms of the present case, they shook their
heads and came to the conclusion that Ichabod
had been carried off by the Galloping Hessian.
As he was a bachelor and in nobody's debt, nobody troubled his head any more about him, the
school was removed to a different quarter of the
hollow and another pedagogue reigned in his
stead.

It is true an old farmer, who had been down
to New York on a visit several years after, and
from whom this account of the ghostly adventure
was received, brought home the intelligence that
Ichabod Crane was still alive; that he had left the
neighborhood, partly through fear of the goblin

and Hans Van Ripper, and partly in mortification at having been suddenly dismissed by the heiress; that he had changed his quarters to a distant part of the country; had kept school and studied law at the same time, had been admitted to the bar, turned politician, electioneered, written for the newspapers, and finally had been made a justice of the Ten Pound Court. Brom Bones too, who shortly after his rival's disappearance conducted the blooming Katrina in triumph to the altar, was observed to look exceedingly knowing whenever the story of Ichabod was related, and always burst into a hearty laugh at the mention of the pumpkin; which led some to suspect that he knew more about the matter than he chose to tell.

The old country wives, however, who are the best judges of these matters, maintain to this day that Ichabod was spirited away by supernatural means; and it is a favorite story often told about the neighborhood round the winter evening fire. The bridge became more than ever an object of superstitious awe, and that may be the reason why the road has been altered of late years, so as to approach the church by the border of the mill-pond. The schoolhouse, being deserted, soon fell to decay, and was reported to be haunted by the ghost of the unfortunate pedagogue; and the plowboy, loitering homeward of a still summer evening, has often fancied his voice at a distance chanting a melancholy psalm tune among the tranquil solitudes of Sleepy Hollow.

Postscript

Found in the
Handwriting of Mr. Knickerbocker

The preceding tale is given almost in the precise words in which I heard it related at a Corporation meeting of the ancient city of Manhattoes, at which were present many of its sagest and most illustrious burghers. The narrator was a pleasant, shabby, gentlemanly old fellow in pepper-and-salt clothes, with a sadly humorous face, and one whom I strongly suspected of being poor, he made such efforts to be entertaining. When his story was concluded there was much laughter and approbation, particularly from two or three deputy aldermen who had been asleep the greatest part of the time. There was, however, one tall, dry-looking old gentleman, with beetling eyebrows, who maintained a grave and rather severe face throughout, now and then folding his arms, inclining his head, and looking down upon the floor, as if turning a doubt over in his mind. He was one of your wary men, who never laugh but upon good grounds—when they have reason and the law on their side. When the mirth of the rest of the company had subsided and silence was restored, he leaned one arm on the elbow of his chair, and sticking the other akimbo, demanded, with a slight but exceedingly sage motion of the head and contraction of the brow, what was the moral of the story and what it went to prove.

The storyteller, who was just putting a glass of wine to his lips as a refreshment after his toils, paused for a moment, looked at his inquirer with an air of infinite deference, and lowering the glass slowly to the table, observed that the story was intended most logically to prove—

"That there is no situation in life but has its advantages and pleasures—provided we will but take a joke as we find it:

"That, therefore, he that runs races with goblin troopers is likely to have rough riding of it.

"Ergo, for a country schoolmaster to be refused the hand of a Dutch heiress is a certain step to high preferment in the state."

The cautious old gentleman knit his brows tenfold closer after this explanation, being sorely puzzled by the ratiocination of the syllogism, while methought the one in pepper-and-salt eyed him with something of a triumphant leer. At length he observed that all this was very well, but still he thought the story a little on the extravagant—there were one or two points on which he had his doubts.

"Faith, sir," replied the storyteller, "as to that matter, I don't believe one-half of it myself."

D. K.

The
SPECTRE
BRIDEGROOM

The
SPECTRE BRIDEGROOM

A TRAVELER'S TALE [1]

He that supper for is dight,
He lyes full cold, I trow, this night!
Yestreen to chamber I him led,
This night Gray Steel has made his bed.
SIR EGER, SIR GRAHAME, AND SIR GRAY STEEL

ON THE SUMMIT of one of the heights of the Odenwald, a wild and romantic tract of Upper Germany, that lies not far from the confluence of the Main and the Rhine, there stood, many, many years since, the Castle of the Baron Von Landshort. It is now quite fallen to decay, and almost buried among beech trees and dark firs; above which, however, its old watchtower may still be seen, struggling, like the former possessor I have mentioned, to carry a high head, and look down upon the neighboring country.

The baron was a dry branch of the great family

[1] The erudite reader well versed in good-for-nothing lore, will perceive that the above tale must have been suggested by a little French anecdote, a circumstance said to have taken place at Paris.

of Katzenellenbogen,[2] and inherited the relics of the property, and all the pride of his ancestors. Though the warlike disposition of his predecessors had much impaired the family possessions, yet the baron still endeavored to keep up some show of former state. The times were peaceable, and the German nobles, in general, had abandoned their inconvenient old castles, perched like eagles' nests among the mountains, and had built more convenient residences in the valleys. Still the baron remained proudly drawn up in his little fortress, cherishing, with hereditary inveteracy, all the old family feuds; so that he was on ill terms with some of his nearest neighbors, on account of disputes that had happened between their great-great-grandfathers.

The baron had but one child, a daughter; but Nature, when she grants but one child, always compensates by making it a prodigy; and so it was with the daughter of the baron. All the nurses, gossips, and country cousins assured her father that she had not her equal for beauty in all Germany; and who should know better than they? She had, moreover, been brought up with great care under the superintendence of two maiden aunts, who had spent some years of their early life at one of the little German courts, and were

[2] *I. e.* CAT'S ELBOW. The name of a family of those parts very powerful in former times. The appellation, we are told, was given in compliment to a peerless dame of the family, celebrated for her fine arm.

skilled in all the branches of knowledge necessary to the education of a fine lady. Under their instructions she became a miracle of accomplishments. By the time she was eighteen, she could embroider to admiration, and had worked whole histories of the saints in tapestry, with such strength of expression in their countenances that they looked like so many souls in purgatory. She could read without great difficulty, and had spelled her way through several church legends, and almost all the chivalric wonders of the Heldenbuch. She had even made considerable proficiency in writing; could sign her own name without missing a letter, and so legibly that her aunts could read it without spectacles. She excelled in making little elegant good-for-nothing ladylike knickknacks of all kinds; was versed in the most abstruse dancing of the day; played a number of airs on the harp and guitar; and knew all the tender ballads of the Minnelieders by heart.

Her aunts, too, having been great flirts and coquettes in their younger days, were admirably calculated to be vigilant guardians and strict censors of the conduct of their niece; for there is no duenna so rigidly prudent, and inexorably decorous, as a superannuated coquette. She was rarely suffered out of their sight; never went beyond the domains of the castle, unless well attended, or rather, well watched; had continual lectures read to her about strict decorum and implicit obedience; and, as to the men—pah!—she was taught to hold them at such a distance, and in such absolute distrust, that, unless properly authorized, she would not have cast a glance upon the handsomest cavalier in the world—no, not if he were even lying at her feet.

The good effects of this system were wonderfully apparent. The young lady was a pattern of docility and correctness. While others were wasting their sweetness in the glare of the world, and liable to be plucked and thrown aside by every hand, she was coyly blooming into fresh and lovely womanhood under the protection of those immaculate spinsters like a rosebud blushing forth among guardian thorns. Her aunts looked upon her with pride and exultation, and vaunted that though all the other young ladies in the world might go astray, yet, thank Heaven, nothing of the kind could happen to the heiress of Katzenellenbogen.

But, however scantily the Baron Von Landshort might be provided with children, his household was by no means a small one; for Providence had enriched him with abundance of poor relations. They, one and all, possessed the affectionate disposition common to humble relatives; were wonderfully attached to the baron, and took every possible occasion to come in swarms and enliven the castle. All family festivals were commemorated by these good people at the baron's expense; and when they were filled with good cheer, they would declare that there was nothing on earth so delightful as these family meetings, these jubilees of the heart.

The baron, though a small man, had a large soul, and it swelled with satisfaction at the consciousness of being the greatest man in the little world about him. He loved to tell long stories about the dark old warriors whose portraits looked grimly down from the walls around, and he found no listeners equal to those who fed at his expense. He was much given to the marvelous, and a firm believer in all those supernatural tales with which every mountain and valley in Germany abounds. The faith of his guests exceeded even his own; they listened to every tale of wonder with open eyes and mouth, and never failed to be astonished, even though repeated for the hundredth time. Thus lived the Baron Von Landshort, the oracle of his table, the absolute monarch of his little territory, and happy, above all things, in the persuasion that he was the wisest man of the age.

At the time of which my story treats, there was a great family gathering at the castle, on an affair of the utmost importance; it was to receive the destined bridegroom of the baron's daughter. A negotiation had been carried on between the father and an old nobleman of Bavaria, to unite the dignity of their houses by the marriage of their children. The preliminaries had been conducted with proper punctilio. The young people were betrothed without seeing each other; and the time was appointed for the marriage ceremony. The young Count Von Altenburg had been recalled from the army for the purpose, and was actually on his way to the baron's to receive his bride. Missives had even been received from him, from Würtzburg, where he was accidentally detained, mentioning the day and hour when he might be expected to arrive.

The castle was in a tumult of preparation to give him a suitable welcome. The fair bride had been decked out with uncommon care. The two aunts had superintended her toilet, and quarreled the whole morning about every article of her dress. The young lady had taken advantage of their contest to follow the bent of her own taste; and fortunately it was a good one. She looked as lovely as youthful bridegroom could desire; and the flutter of expectation heightened the lustre of her charms.

The suffusions that mantled her face and neck, the gentle heaving of the bosom, the eye now and then lost in reverie, all betrayed the soft tumult that was going on in her little heart. The aunts were continually hovering around her; for maiden aunts are apt to take great interest in affairs of this nature. They were giving her a world of staid counsel how to deport herself, what to say, and in what manner to receive the expected lover.

The baron was no less busied in preparations. He had, in truth, nothing exactly to do; but he

was naturally a fuming, bustling little man, and
could not remain passive when all the world was
in a hurry. He worried from top to bottom of the
castle with an air of infinite anxiety; he continually called the servants from their work to exhort
them to be diligent; and buzzed about every hall
and chamber, as idly restless and importunate as
a bluebottle fly on a warm summer's day.

In the meantime the fatted calf had been
killed; the forests had rung with the clamor of
the huntsmen; the kitchen was crowded with
good cheer; the cellars had yielded up whole
oceans of *Rhein-wein,* and *Ferne-wein;* and even
the great Heidelberg tun had been laid under
contribution. Everything was ready to receive the
distinguished guest with *Saus und Braus* in the
true spirit of German hospitality—but the guest
delayed to make his appearance. Hour rolled
after hour. The sun, that had poured his down-
ward rays upon the rich forest of the Odenwald,
now just gleamed along the summits of the mountains. The baron mounted the highest tower and
strained his eyes in hope of catching a distant
sight of the count and his attendants. Once he
thought he beheld them; the sound of horns came
floating from the valley, prolonged by the mountain echoes. A number of horsemen were seen far
below, slowly advancing along the road; but when
they had nearly reached the foot of the mountain,
they suddenly struck off in a different direction.
The last ray of sunshine departed—the bats began

to flit by in the twilight—the road grew dimmer and dimmer to the view, and nothing appeared stirring in it but now and then a peasant lagging homeward from his labor.

While the old castle of Landshort was in this state of perplexity, a very interesting scene was transacting in a different part of the Odenwald.

The young Count Von Altenburg was tranquilly pursuing his route in that sober jog-trot way in which a man travels toward matrimony when his friends have taken all the trouble and uncertainty of courtship off his hands, and a bride is waiting for him, as certainly as a dinner at the end of his journey. He had encountered at Würtzburg a youthful companion in arms, with whom he had seen some service on the frontiers—Herman Von Starkenfaust, one of the stoutest hands and worthiest hearts of German chivalry, who was now returning from the army. His father's castle was not far distant from the old fortress of Landshort, although an hereditary feud rendered the families hostile, and strangers to each other.

In the warm-hearted moment of recognition, the young friends related all their past adventures and fortunes, and the count gave the whole history of his intended nuptials with a young lady whom he had never seen, but of whose charms he had received the most enrapturing descriptions.

As the route of the friends lay in the same direction, they agreed to perform the rest of their journey together; and, that they might do it more leisurely, set off from Würtzburg at an early hour, the count having given directions for his retinue to follow and overtake him.

They beguiled their wayfaring with recollections of their military scenes and adventures; but the count was apt to be a little tedious, now and then, about the reputed charms of his bride, and the felicity that awaited him.

In this way they had entered among the mountains of the Odenwald, and were traversing one of its most lonely and thickly wooded passes. It is well known that the forests of Germany have always been as much infested by robbers as its castles by spectres; and, at this time, the former were particularly numerous, from the hordes of disbanded soldiers wandering about the country. It will not appear extraordinary, therefore, that the cavaliers were attacked by a gang of these stragglers, in the midst of the forest. They defended themselves with bravery, but were nearly overpowered, when the count's retinue arrived to their assistance. At sight of them the robbers fled, but not until the count had received a mortal wound. He was slowly and carefully conveyed back to the city of Würtzburg, and a friar summoned from a neighboring convent, who was famous for his skill in administering to both soul and body; but half of his skill was superfluous; the moments of the unfortunate count were numbered.

With his dying breath he entreated his friend

to repair instantly to the castle of Landshort and explain the fatal cause of his not keeping his appointment with his bride. Though not the most ardent of lovers, he was one of the most punctilious of men, and appeared earnestly solicitous that his mission should be speedily and courteously executed. "Unless this is done," said he, "I shall not sleep quietly in my grave!" He repeated these last words with peculiar solemnity. A request, at a moment so impressive, admitted no hesitation. Starkenfaust endeavored to soothe him to calmness; promised faithfully to execute his wish, and gave him his hand in solemn pledge. The dying man pressed it in acknowledgment, but soon lapsed into delirium—raved about his bride—his engagements—his plighted word; ordered his horse, that he might ride to the castle of Landshort; and expired in the fancied act of vaulting into the saddle.

Starkenfaust bestowed a sigh and a soldier's tear on the untimely fate of his comrade; and then pondered on the awkward mission he had undertaken. His heart was heavy, and his head perplexed; for he was to present himself an unbidden guest among hostile people, and to damp their festivity with tidings fatal to their hopes. Still there were certain whisperings of curiosity in his bosom to see this far-famed beauty of Katzenellenbogen so cautiously shut up from the world; for he was a passionate admirer of the sex, and there was a dash of eccentricity and enterprise in his character that made him fond of all singular adventure.

Previous to his departure he made all due arrangements with the holy fraternity of the convent for the funeral solemnities of his friend, who was to be buried in the cathedral of Würtzburg, near some of his illustrious relatives; and the mourning retinue of the count took charge of his remains.

It is now high time that we should return to the ancient family of Katzenellenbogen, who were impatient for their guest, and still more for their dinner; and to the worthy little baron, whom we left airing himself on the watchtower.

Night closed in, but still no guest arrived. The baron descended from the tower in despair. The banquet, which had been delayed from hour to hour, could no longer be postponed. The meats were already overdone; the cook in an agony; and the whole household had the look of a garrison that had been reduced by famine. The baron was obliged reluctantly to give orders for the feast without the presence of the guest. All were seated at the table, and just on the point of commencing, when the sound of a horn from without the gate gave notice of the approach of a stranger. Another long blast filled the old courts of the castle with its echoes, and was answered by the warder from the walls. The baron hastened to receive his future son-in-law.

The drawbridge had been let down, and the

The drawbridge had been let down and the stranger
was before the gate

stranger was before the gate. He was a tall, gallant cavalier, mounted on a black steed. His countenance was pale, but he had a beaming, romantic eye, and an air of stately melancholy. The baron was a little mortified that he should have come in this simple, solitary style. His dignity for a moment was ruffled, and he felt disposed to consider it a want of proper respect for the important occasion, and the important family with which he was to be connected. He pacified himself, however, with the conclusion, that it must have been youthful impatience which had induced him thus to spur on sooner than his attendants.

"I am sorry," said the stranger, "to break in upon you thus unseasonably——"

Here the baron interrupted him with a world of compliments and greetings; for, to tell the truth, he prided himself upon his courtesy and eloquence. The stranger attempted, once or twice, to stem the torrent of words, but in vain, so he bowed his head and suffered it to flow on. By the time the baron had come to a pause, they had reached the inner court of the castle; and the stranger was again about to speak, when he was once more interrupted by the appearance of the female part of the family, leading forth the shrinking and blushing bride. He gazed on her for a moment as one entranced. It seemed as if his whole soul beamed forth in the gaze, and rested upon that lovely form. One of the maiden aunts whispered something in her ear; she made an effort to speak; her moist blue eye was timidly raised; gave a shy glance of inquiry on the stranger; and was cast again to the ground. The words died away; but there was a sweet smile playing about her lips, and a soft dimpling of the cheek that showed her glance had not been unsatisfactory. It was impossible for a girl of the fond age of eighteen, highly predisposed for love and matrimony, not to be pleased with so gallant a cavalier.

The late hour at which the guest had arrived left no time for parley. The baron was peremptory, and deferred all particular conversation until the morning, and led the way to the untasted banquet.

It was served up in the great hall of the castle. Around the walls hung the hard-favored portraits of the heroes of the house of Katzenellenbogen, and the trophies which they had gained in the field and in the chase. Hacked corselets, splintered jousting spears, and tattered banners were mingled with the spoils of sylvan warfare; the jaws of the wolf and the tusks of the boar grinned horribly among crossbows and battle-axes, and a huge pair of antlers branched immediately over the head of the youthful bridegroom.

The cavalier took but little notice of the company or the entertainment. He scarcely tasted the banquet, but seemed absorbed in admiration of his bride. He conversed in a low tone that could not be overheard—for the language of love is never loud; but where is the female ear so dull that it cannot catch the softest whisper of the lover? There was a mingled tenderness and gravity in his manner, that appeared to have a powerful effect upon the young lady. Her color came and went as she listened with deep attention. Now and then she made some blushing reply, and when his eye was turned away, she would steal a side-long glance at his romantic countenance, and heave a gentle sigh of tender happiness. It was evident that the young couple were completely enamored. The aunts, who were deeply versed in the mysteries of the heart, declared that they had fallen in love with each other at first sight.

The feast went on merrily, or at least noisily, for the guests were all blessed with those keen appetites that attend upon light purses and mountain air. The baron told his best and longest stories, and never had he told them so well, or with such great effect. If there was anything marvelous, his auditors were lost in astonishment; and if anything facetious, they were sure to laugh exactly in the right place. The baron, it is true, like most great men, was too dignified to utter any joke but a dull one; it was always enforced, how-ever, by a bumper of excellent Hockheimer; and even a dull joke, at one's own table, served up with jolly old wine, is irresistible. Many good things were said by poorer and keener wits, that would not bear repeating, except on similar oc-

casions; many sly speeches whispered in ladies'
ears, that almost convulsed them with suppressed
laughter; and a song or two roared out by a poor,
but merry and broad-faced cousin of the baron,
that absolutely made the maiden aunts hold up
their fans.

Amidst all this revelry, the stranger guest maintained a most singular and unseasonable gravity.
His countenance assumed a deeper cast of dejec-
tion as the evening advanced; and, strange as it
may appear, even the baron's jokes seemed only
to render him the more melancholy. At times he
was lost in thought, and at times there was a
perturbed and restless wandering of the eye that
bespoke a mind but ill at ease. His conversations
with the bride became more and more earnest
and mysterious. Lowering clouds began to steal
over the fair serenity of her brow, and tremors
to run through her tender frame.

All this could not escape the notice of the company. Their gaiety was chilled by the unaccount-
able gloom of the bridegroom; their spirits were
infected; whispers and glances were inter-
changed, accompanied by shrugs and dubious
shakes of the head. The song and the laugh grew
less and less frequent; there were dreary pauses
in the conversation, which were at length succeeded by wild tales and supernatural legends.
One dismal story produced another still more dismal, and the baron nearly frightened some of the
ladies into hysterics with the history of the

goblin horseman that carried away the fair Leonora; a dreadful story, which has since been put into excellent verse, and is read and believed by all the world.

The bridegroom listened to this tale with profound attention. He kept his eyes steadily fixed on the baron, and, as the story drew to a close, began gradually to rise from his seat, growing taller and taller, until, in the baron's entranced eye, he seemed almost to tower into a giant. The moment the tale was finished, he heaved a deep sigh, and took a solemn farewell of the company. They were all amazement. The baron was perfectly thunderstruck.

What! Going to leave the castle at midnight? Why, everything was prepared for his reception. A chamber was ready for him if he wished to retire.

The stranger shook his head mournfully and mysteriously. "I must lay my head in a different chamber tonight!"

There was something in this reply, and the tone in which it was uttered, that made the baron's heart misgive him; but he rallied his forces, and repeated his hospitable entreaties.

The stranger shook his head silently, but positively, at every offer; and, waving his farewell to the company, stalked slowly out of the hall. The maiden aunts were absolutely petrified; the bride hung her head, and a tear stole to her eye.

The baron followed the stranger to the great

court of the castle, where the black charger stood pawing the earth and snorting with impatience. When they had reached the portal, whose deep archway was dimly lighted by a cresset, the stranger paused, and addressed the baron in a hollow tone of voice, which the vaulted roof rendered still more sepulchral.

"Now that we are alone," said he, "I will impart to you the reason of my going. I have a solemn, an indispensable engagement—"

"Why," said the baron, "cannot you send someone in your place?"

"It admits of no substitute—I must attend it in person—I must away to Würtzburg Cathedral—"

"Ay," said the baron, plucking up spirit, "but not until tomorrow—tomorrow you shall take your bride there."

"No! no!" replied the stranger, with tenfold solemnity, "my engagement is with no bride—the worms! the worms expect me! I am a dead man— I have been slain by robbers—my body lies at Würtzburg—at midnight I am to be buried—the grave is waiting for me—I must keep my appointment!"

He sprang on his black charger, dashed over the drawbridge, and the clattering of his horse's hoofs was lost in the whistling of the night-blast.

The baron returned to the hall in the utmost consternation, and related what had passed. Two ladies fainted outright, others sickened at the idea of having banqueted with a spectre. It was the

opinion of some that this might be the wild hunts-
man, famous in German legend. Some talked of
mountain sprites, of wood-demons, and of other
supernatural beings, with which the good people
of Germany have been so grievously harassed
since time immemorial. One of the poor relations
ventured to suggest that it might be some sportive
evasion of the young cavalier, and that the very
gloominess of the caprice seemed to accord with
so melancholy a personage. This, however, drew
on him the indignation of the whole company,
and especially the baron, who looked upon him
as little better than an infidel; so that he was fain
to abjure his heresy as speedily as possible, and
come into the faith of the true believers.

But whatever may have been the doubts en-
tertained, they were completely put to an end by
the arrival, next day, of regular missives, confirm-
ing the intelligence of the young count's murder,
and his interment in Würtzburg Cathedral.

The dismay at the castle may well be imagined.
The baron shut himself up in his chamber. The
guests, who had come to rejoice with him, could
not think of abandoning him in his distress. They
wandered about the courts, or collected in groups
in the hall, shaking their heads and shrugging their
shoulders, at the troubles of so good a man; and
sat longer than ever at table, and ate and drank
more stoutly than ever, by way of keeping up
their spirits. But the situation of the widowed
bride was the most pitiable. To have lost a hus-

band before she had even embraced him—and such a husband! If the very spectre could be so gracious and noble, what must have been the living man! She filled the house with lamentations.

On the night of the second day of her widowhood, she had retired to her chamber, accompanied by one of her aunts, who insisted on sleeping with her. The aunt, who was one of the best tellers of ghost stories in all Germany, had just been recounting one of her longest, and had fallen asleep in the very midst of it. The chamber was remote, and overlooked a small garden. The niece lay pensively gazing at the beams of the rising moon, as they trembled on the leaves of an aspen tree before the lattice. The castle clock had just tolled midnight, when a soft strain of music stole up from the garden. She rose hastily from her bed, and stepped lightly to the window. A tall figure stood among the shadows of the trees. As it raised its head, a beam of moonlight fell upon the countenance. Heaven and earth! She beheld the Spectre Bridegroom! A loud shriek at that moment burst upon her ear, and her aunt, who had been awakened by the music, and had followed her silently to the window, fell into her arms. When she looked again, the spectre had disappeared.

Of the two females, the aunt now required the most soothing, for she was perfectly beside herself with terror. As to the young lady, there was

*Heaven and earth! She beheld the Spectre
Bridegroom!*

something, even in the spectre of her lover, that seemed endearing. There was still the semblance of manly beauty; and though the shadow of a man is but little calculated to satisfy the affections of a lovesick girl, yet, where the substance is not to be had, even that is consoling. The aunt declared she would never sleep in that chamber again. The niece, for once, was refractory and declared as strongly that she would sleep in no other in the castle: the consequence was, that she had to sleep in it alone; but she drew a promise from her aunt not to relate the story of the spectre, lest she should be denied the only melancholy pleasure left her on earth—that of inhabiting the chamber over which the guardian shade of her lover kept its nightly vigils.

How long the good old lady would have observed this promise is uncertain, for she dearly loved to talk of the marvelous, and there is a triumph in being the first to tell a frightful story; it is, however, still quoted in the neighborhood, as a memorable instance of female secrecy, that she kept it to herself for a whole week; when she was suddenly absolved from all further restraint, by intelligence brought to the breakfast table one morning that the young lady was not to be found. Her room was empty—the bed had not been slept in—the window was open, and the bird had flown!

The astonishment and concern with which the intelligence was received can only be imagined by those who have witnessed the agitation which the mishaps of a great man cause among his friends. Even the poor relations paused for a moment from the indefatigable labors of the trencher; when the aunt, who had at first been struck speechless, wrung her hands and shrieked out, "The goblin! The goblin! She's carried away by the goblin!"

In a few words she related the fearful scene of the garden, and concluded that the spectre must have carried off his bride. Two of the domestics corroborated the opinion, for they had heard the clattering of a horse's hoofs down the mountain about midnight, and had no doubt that it was the spectre on his black charger, bearing her away to the tomb. All present were struck with the direful probability; for events of the kind are extremely common in Germany, as many well-authenticated histories bear witness.

What a lamentable situation was that of the poor baron! What a heart-rending dilemma for a fond father, and a member of the great family of Katzenellenbogen! His only daughter had either been rapt away to the grave, or he was to have some wood-demon for a son-in-law, and, perchance, a troop of goblin grandchildren. As usual, he was completely bewildered, and all the castle in an uproar. The men were ordered to take horse, and scour every road and path and glen of the Odenwald. The baron himself had just drawn on his jack-boots, girded on his sword, and was about to mount his steed to sally forth on the doubtful quest, when he was brought to a pause by a new apparition. A lady was seen approaching the castle, mounted on a palfrey, attended by a cavalier on horseback. She galloped up to the gate, sprang from her horse, and falling at the baron's feet, embraced his knees. It was his lost daughter, and her companion—the Spectre Bridegroom! The baron was astounded. He looked at his daughter, then at the spectre, and almost doubted the evidence of his senses. The latter, too, was wonderfully improved in his appearance since his visit to the world of spirits. His dress was splendid, and set off a noble figure of manly symmetry. He was no longer pale and melancholy. His fine countenance was flushed with the glow of youth, and joy rioted in his large dark eye.

The mystery was soon cleared up. The cavalier (for, in truth, as you must have known all the while, he was no goblin) announced himself as Sir Herman Von Starkenfaust. He related his adventure with the young count. He told how he had hastened to the castle to deliver the unwelcome tidings, but that the eloquence of the baron had interrupted him in every attempt to tell his tale. How the sight of the bride had completely captivated him, and that to pass a few hours near her, he had tacitly suffered the mistake to continue. How he had been sorely perplexed in what way to make a decent retreat, until the baron's goblin stories had suggested his eccentric exit.

How, fearing the feudal hostility of the family, he had repeated his visits by stealth—had haunted the garden beneath the young lady's window—had wooed—had won—had borne away in triumph—and, in a word, had wedded the fair.

Under any other circumstances the baron would have been inflexible, for he was tenacious of paternal authority, and devoutly obstinate in all family feuds. But he loved his daughter; he had lamented her as lost; he rejoiced to find her still alive; and, though her husband was of a hostile house, yet, thank Heaven, he was not a goblin. There was something, it must be acknowledged, that did not exactly accord with his notions of strict veracity, in the joke the knight had passed upon him of his being a dead man. But several old friends present, who had served in the wars, assured him that every stratagem was excusable in love, and that the cavalier was entitled to especial privilege, having lately served as a trooper.

Matters, therefore, were happily arranged. The baron pardoned the young couple on the spot. The revels at the castle were resumed. The poor relations overwhelmed this new member of the family with loving kindness. He was so gallant, so generous—and so rich. The aunts, it is true, were somewhat scandalized that their system of strict seclusion and passive obedience should be so badly exemplified, but attributed it all to their negligence in not having the windows grated. One of them was particularly mortified at having her marvelous story marred, and that the only spectre she had ever seen should turn out a counterfeit. But the niece seemed perfectly happy at having found him substantial flesh and blood—and so the story ends.

The
MOOR'S LEGACY

The
MOOR'S LEGACY

1.

JUST WITHIN THE fortress of the Al-
hambra, in front of the royal palace, is the little
park of the cisterns where reservoirs of water,
hidden from sight, have existed from the time of
the Moors. At one corner is a Moorish well, cut
through the living rock to a great depth, the water
of which is cold as ice and clear as crystal. It is
famous throughout Granada; and water carriers,
some bearing great water jars on their shoulders,
others driving donkeys laden with earthen vessels,
ascend and descend the steep, woody avenues of
the Alhambra from early dawn until late at night.

Among the water carriers who once resorted to
this well there was a sturdy, strong-backed,
bandy-legged little fellow named Pedro Gil, but
called Peregil for shortness. He was a Gallego, or

native of Gallicia. Nature seems to have formed races of men as she has species of animals for different kinds of drudgery. In France the shoe-blacks are all Savoyards, the porters of hotels all Swiss. So in Spain the carriers of water and bearers of burdens are all sturdy little natives of Gallicia. No man says, "Get me a porter," but, "Call a Gallego."

Peregil the Gallego had begun business with merely a great earthen jar, which he carried upon his shoulder. By degrees he rose in the world, and was enabled to purchase a stout shaggy-haired donkey. On each side of this, his long-eared helper, in a kind of pannier, were slung his water jars covered with fig leaves to protect them from the sun. There was not a more industrious water carrier in all Granada, nor one more merry withal. The streets rang with his cheerful voice as he trudged after his donkey, singing: "Who wants water—water colder than snow—who wants water from the well of the Alhambra—cold as ice and clear as crystal?"

When he served a customer with a sparkling glass, it was always with a pleasant word that caused a smile. Thus Peregil the Gallego was noted throughout all Granada for being one of the pleasantest and happiest of mortals.

Yet it is not he who sings loudest and jokes most that has the lightest heart. Under all this air of merriment, honest Peregil had his cares and troubles.

He had a large family of ragged children to support, who were hungry and clamorous as a nest of young swallows, and beset him with their outcries for food whenever he came home in the evening. He had a helpmate, too, who was anything but a help to him. She had been a village beauty before marriage, noted for her skill in dancing the bolero and rattling the castanets, and she still retained her early propensities, spending the hard earnings of honest Peregil in frippery, and laying the very donkey under requisition for junketing parties into the country on Sundays, and saints' days, and those innumerable holidays which are rather more numerous in Spain than the days of the week. With all this she was a little of a slattern, something more of a lie-a-bed, and, above all, a gossip of the first order; neglecting house, household, and everything else, to loiter slipshod in the houses of her gossipy neighbors.

Peregil bore all the heavy dispensations of wife and children with as meek a spirit as his donkey bore the water jars; and, however he might shake his ears in private, never ventured to question the household virtues of his slatternly spouse.

He loved his children, too, even as an owl loves its owlets, seeing in them his own image multiplied and perpetuated, for they were a sturdy, long-backed, bandy-legged little brood. The great pleasure of honest Peregil was, whenever he could afford himself a scanty holiday, to take the whole litter with him, some in his arms, some tugging at his skirts, and some trudging at his heels, and to treat them to a gambol among the orchards of the Vega.

It was a late hour one summer night, and most of the water carriers had stopped their toils. The day had been uncommonly sultry; the night was one of those delicious moonlights, which tempt the inhabitants of those southern climes to indemnify themselves for the heat and inaction of the day by lingering in the open air and enjoying its tempered sweetness until after midnight. Customers for water were therefore still abroad. Peregil, like a considerate, painstaking little father, thought of his hungry children.

"One more journey to the well," said he to himself, "to earn a good Sunday's *puchero* for the little ones."

So saying, he trudged rapidly up the steep avenue of the Alhambra, singing as he went.

Arriving at the well, he found it deserted by everyone except a solitary stranger in Moorish garb, seated on the stone bench in the moonlight. Peregil paused at first, and regarded him with surprise, not unmixed with awe, but the Moor feebly beckoned him to approach.

"I am faint and ill," said he. "Aid me to return to the city, and I will pay thee double what thou couldst gain by thy jars of water."

The honest heart of the little water carrier was touched with compassion at the appeal of the stranger. "God forbid," said he, "that I should ask fee or reward for doing a common act of humanity."

He accordingly helped the Moor on his donkey, and set off slowly for Granada, the poor Moslem being so weak that it was necessary to hold him on the animal to keep him from falling to the earth.

When they entered the city, the water carrier demanded whither he should conduct him. "Alas!" said the Moor faintly, "I have neither home nor habitation. I am a stranger in the land. Suffer me to lay my head this night beneath thy roof, and thou shalt be amply repaid."

Honest Peregil thus saw himself unexpectedly saddled with an infidel guest, but he was too humane to refuse a night's shelter to a fellow being in so forlorn a plight; so he conducted the Moor to his dwelling. The children, who had sallied forth, open-mouthed as usual, on hearing the tramp of the donkey, ran back with fright, when they beheld the turbaned stranger, and hid themselves behind their mother. The latter stepped forth intrepidly, like a ruffling hen before her brood, when a vagrant dog approaches.

"What infidel companion," cried she, "is this you have brought home at this late hour, to draw upon us the eyes of the Inquisition?"

"Be quiet, wife," replied the Gallego. "Here is a poor sick stranger, without friend or home. Wouldst thou turn him forth to perish in the streets?"

*"What infidel companion," cried she, "is this you have
brought home?"*

The wife would still have remonstrated, for, though she lived in a hovel, she was a furious stickler for the credit of her house. The little water carrier, however, for once was stiff-necked, and refused to bend beneath the yoke. He assisted the poor Moslem to alight, and spread a mat and a sheepskin for him, on the ground, in the coolest part of the house; being the only kind of bed that his poverty afforded.

In a little while the Moor was seized with violent convulsions, which defied all the ministering skill of the simple water carrier. The eye of the poor patient acknowledged his kindness. During an interval of his fits he called him to his side, and addressed him in a low voice. "My end," said he, "I fear is at hand. If I die I bequeath you this box as a reward for your charity." So saying, he opened his cloak and showed a small box of sandalwood, strapped around his body.

"God grant, my friend," replied the worthy little Gallego, "that you may live many years to enjoy your treasure, whatever it may be."

The Moor shook his head; he laid his hand upon the box, and would have said something more concerning it, but his convulsions returned with increased violence, and in a little while he expired.

The water carrier's wife was now as one distracted. "This comes," said she, "of your foolish good nature, always running into scrapes to oblige others. What will become of us when this corpse is found in our house? We shall be sent to prison as murderers."

Poor Peregil was in equal tribulation, and almost repented himself of having done a good deed. At length a thought struck him. "It is not yet day," said he. "I can convey the dead body out of the city and bury it in the sands on the banks of the Xenil. No one saw the Moor enter our dwelling, and no one will know anything of his death." So said, so done. The wife aided him; they rolled the body of the unfortunate Moslem in the mat on which he had expired, laid it across the ass, and set out with it for the banks of the river.

2.

As ill luck would have it, there lived opposite to the water carrier a barber named Pedrillo Pedrugo, one of the most prying, tattling, mischief-making men of his gossipy tribe. He was a weasel-faced, spider-legged varlet, supple and insinuating; the famous Barber of Seville could not surpass him for his universal knowledge of the affairs of others, and he had no more power of retention than a sieve. It was said that he slept with one eye at a time, and kept one ear uncovered, so that, even in his sleep, he might see and hear all that was going on. Certain it is, he was a sort of scandalous chronicle for the busybodies of

Granada, and had more customers than all the rest of his fraternity.

This meddlesome barber heard Peregil arrive at an unusual hour of night, and the exclamation of his wife and children. His head was instantly popped out of a little window which served him as a lookout, and he saw his neighbor assist a man in a Moorish garb into his dwelling. This was so strange an occurrence that Pedrillo Pedrugo slept not a wink that night—every five minutes he was at his loophole, watching the lights that gleamed through the chinks of his neighbor's door, and before daylight he beheld Peregil sally forth with his donkey unusually laden.

The inquisitive barber was in a fidget; he slipped on his clothes, and, stealing forth silently, followed the water carrier at a distance, until he saw him dig a hole in the sandy bank of the Xenil, and bury something that had the appearance of a dead body.

The barber hied himself home and fidgeted about his shop, setting everything upside down, until sunrise. He then took a basin under his arm, and sallied forth to the house of his daily customer, the Alcalde, or Mayor.

The Alcalde had just risen. Pedrillo Pedrugo seated him in a chair, threw a napkin round his neck, put a basin of hot water under his chin, and began to mollify his beard with his fingers.

"Strange doings," said Pedrugo, who played barber and newsmonger at the same time.

"Strange doings! Robbery, and murder, and burial, all in one night!"

"Hey? How! What is it you say?" cried the Alcalde.

"I say," replied the barber, rubbing a piece of soap over the nose and mouth of the dignitary, for a Spanish barber disdains to employ a brush; "I say that Peregil the Gallego has robbed and murdered a Moorish Mussulman, and buried him this blessed night."

"But how do you know all this?" demanded the Alcalde.

"Be patient, Señor, and you shall hear all about it," replied Pedrillo, taking him by the nose and sliding a razor over his cheek. He then recounted all that he had seen, going through both operations at the same time, shaving his beard, washing his chin, and wiping him dry with a dirty napkin, while he related the robbing, murdering, and burying of the Moslem.

Now it so happened that this Alcalde was one of the most overbearing, and at the same time most gripping and corrupt curmudgeons in all Granada. It could not be denied, however, that he set a high value upon justice, for he sold it at its weight in gold. He presumed the case in point to be one of murder and robbery; doubtless there must be rich spoil; how was it to be secured by the legitimate hands of the law? For as to merely entrapping the delinquent—that would be feeding the gallows; but entrapping the booty—that would be enriching the judge; and such, according to his creed, was the great end of justice. So thinking, he summoned to his presence his trustiest police officer: a gaunt, hungry-looking varlet, clad, according to the custom of his order, in the ancient Spanish garb—a broad black beaver, turned up at the sides; a quaint ruff, a small black cloak dangling from his shoulders; rusty black underclothes that set off his spare wiry form; while in his hand he bore a slender white wand, the dreaded insigne of his office. Such was the legal bloodhound of the ancient Spanish breed that he put upon the traces of the unlucky water carrier; and such was his speed and certainty that he was upon the haunches of poor Peregil before the latter had returned to his dwelling, and brought both him and his donkey before the dispenser of justice.

The Alcalde bent upon him one of his most terrific frowns. "Hark ye, culprit," roared he in a voice that made the knees of the little Gallego smite together—"Hark ye, culprit! There is no need of denying thy guilt: everything is known to me. A gallows is the proper reward for the crime thou hast committed, but I am merciful, and readily listen to reason. The man that has been murdered in thy house was a Moor, an infidel, the enemy of our faith. It was doubtless in a fit of religious zeal that thou hast slain him. I will be indulgent, therefore; render up the property of which thou hast robbed him, and we will hush the matter up."

The poor water carrier called upon all the saints

to witness his innocence; alas! not one of them appeared, and if there had, the Alcalde would not have believed him. The water carrier related the whole story of the dying Moor with the straightforward simplicity of truth, but it was all in vain.

"Wilst thou persist in saying," demanded the judge, "that this Moslem had neither gold nor jewels, which were the object of thy cupidity?"

"As I hope to be saved, your worship," replied the water carrier, "he had nothing but a small box of sandalwood, which he bequeathed to me in reward of my services."

"A box of sandalwood! A box of sandalwood!" exclaimed the Alcalde, his eyes sparkling at the idea of precious jewels. "And where is this box? Where have you concealed it?"

"An' it please your grace," replied the water carrier, "it is in one of the panniers of my mule, and heartily at the service of your worship."

He had hardly spoken the words when the keen police officer darted off and reappeared in an instant with the mysterious box of sandalwood. The Alcalde opened it with an eager and trembling hand; all pressed forward to gaze upon the treasures it was expected to contain; when, to their disappointment, nothing appeared within but a parchment scroll, covered with Arabic characters, and an end of a waxen taper!

When there is nothing to be gained by the conviction of a prisoner, justice, even in Spain, is apt to be impartial. The Alcalde, having recovered from his disappointment and found there was really no booty in the case, now listened dispassionately to the explanation of the water carrier, which was corroborated by the testimony of his wife. Being convinced, therefore, of his innocence, he discharged him from arrest; nay more, he permitted him to carry off the Moor's legacy, the box of sandalwood and its contents, as the well-merited reward of his humanity; but he retained his donkey in payment of cost and charges.

3.

Behold the unfortunate little Gallego reduced once more to the necessity of being his own water carrier, and trudging up to the well of the Alhambra with a great earthen jar upon his shoulder. As he toiled up the hill in the heat of a summer noon his usual good humor forsook him.

"Dog of an Alcalde!" would he cry, "to rob a poor man of the means of his subsistence—of the best friend he had in the world!" And then, at the remembrance of the beloved companion of his labors, all the kindness of his nature would break forth. "Ah, donkey of my heart!" would he exclaim, resting his burden on a stone, and wiping the sweat from his brow. "Ah, donkey of my heart! I warrant me thou thinkest of thy old master! I warrant me thou missest the water jars—poor beast!"

To add to his afflictions his wife received him,

on his return home, with whimperings and repin-
ings. She had clearly the upper hand, having
warned him not to commit the act of hospitality
that had brought on him all these misfortunes,
and like a knowing woman, she took every occasion to remind him of it. If ever her children lacked
food, or needed a new garment, she would answer
with a sneer, "Go to your father; he's heir to King
Chico of Alhambra. Ask him to help you out of the
Moor's strongbox."

At length one evening, when, after a hot day's
toil, she taunted him in the usual manner, he lost
all patience. He did not venture to retort, but his
eye rested upon the box of sandalwood, which lay
on a shelf with lid half open, as if laughing in
mockery of his vexation. Seizing it up, he dashed
it with indignation on the floor.

"Unlucky was the day that I ever set eyes on
thee," he cried, "or sheltered thy master beneath
my roof."

As the box struck the floor the lid flew wide
open, and the parchment scroll rolled forth. Peregil sat regarding the scroll for some time in moody
silence. At length rallying his ideas, "Who knows,"
thought he, "but this writing may be of some importance, as the Moor seems to have guarded it
with such care." Picking it up, therefore, he put it
in his bosom, and the next morning, as he was
crying water through the streets, he stopped at the
shop of a Moor, a native of Tangiers, who sold

trinkets and perfumery, and asked him to explain the contents.

The Moor read the scroll attentively, then stroked his beard and smiled. "This manuscript," said he, "is a form of incantation for the recovery of hidden treasure, that is under the power of enchantment. It is said to have such virtue that the strongest bolts and bars, nay rock itself, will yield before it."

"Bah!" cried the little Gallego. "What is all that to me? I am no enchanter, and know nothing of buried treasure." So saying he shouldered his water jar, left the scroll in the hands of the Moor, and trudged forward on his daily rounds.

That evening, however, as he rested himself at the well of the Alhambra, he found a number of gossips assembled at the place, and their conversation, as is not unusual at that shadowy hour, turned upon old tales and traditions of a supernatural nature. Being all poor as rats, they dwelt with peculiar fondness upon the popular theme of enchanted riches left by the Moors in various parts of the Alhambra. Above all, they concurred in the belief that there were great treasures buried deep in the earth under the tower of the Seven Floors.

These stories made an unusual impression on the mind of honest Peregil, and they sank deeper and deeper into his thoughts as he returned alone down the darkling avenues. "What if, after all,

there should be treasure hid beneath that tower—
and if the scroll I left with the Moor should enable
me to get at it!"

That night he tumbled and tossed, and could
scarcely get a wink of sleep for the thoughts that
were bewildering his brain. In the morning, bright
and early, he went to the shop of the Moor, and
told him all that was passing in his mind.

"You can read Arabic," said he. "Suppose we go
together to the tower and try the effect of the
charm; if it fails we are no worse off than before,
but if it succeeds we will share equally all the
treasure we may discover."

"Hold," replied the Moslem, "this writing is not
sufficient of itself. It must be read at midnight, by
the light of a taper singularly compounded and
prepared, the ingredients of which are not within
my reach. Without such a taper the scroll is of no
use."

"Say no more!" cried the little Gallego. "I have
such a taper at hand and will bring it here in a
moment." So saying he hastened home, and soon
returned with the end of a yellow wax taper that
he had found in the box of sandalwood. The Moor
felt it, and smelled of it. "Here are rare and costly
perfumes," said he, "combined with this yellow
wax. This is the kind of taper specified in the
scroll. While this burns, the strongest walls and
most secret caverns will remain open; woe to him,
however, who lingers within until it be extin-

guished. He will remain enchanted with the treasure."

It was now agreed between them to try the
charm that very night. At a late hour, therefore,
when nothing was stirring but bats and owls, they
ascended the woody hill of the Alhambra, and approached that awful tower, shrouded by trees and
rendered formidable by so many traditionary
tales.

By the light of a lantern, they groped their way
through bushes, and over fallen stones, to the
door of a vault beneath the tower. With fear and
trembling they descended a flight of steps cut into
the rock. It led to an empty chamber, damp and
drear, from which another flight of steps led to a
deeper vault. In this way they descended four
flights, leading into as many vaults, one below the
other, but the floor of the fourth was solid, and
though, according to tradition, there remained
three vaults still below, it was said to be impossible
to penetrate farther.

The air of this vault was damp and chilly, and
had an earthy smell, and the light scarce cast forth
any rays. They paused here for a time in breath-
less suspense, until they faintly heard the clock of
the watchtower strike midnight; upon this they
lit the waxen taper, which diffused an odor of
myrrh, and frankincense, and storax.

The Moor began to read in a hurried voice. He
had scarce finished, when there was a noise as of

The floor yawning open disclosed a flight of steps

subterraneous thunder. The earth shook, and the floor yawning open disclosed a flight of steps. Trembling with awe, they descended, and by the light of the lantern found themselves in another vault, covered with Arabic inscriptions. In the center stood a great chest, secured with seven bands of steel, at each end of which sat an enchanted Moor in armor, but motionless as a statue, being controlled by the power of the incantation. Before the chest were several jars filled with gold and silver and precious stones. In the largest of these they thrust their arms up to the elbow, and at every dip hauled forth handfuls of broad yellow pieces of Moorish gold, or bracelets and ornaments of the same precious metal, while occasionally a necklace of oriental pearl would stick to their fingers. Still they trembled and breathed short while cramming their pockets with the spoils; and cast many a fearful glance at the two enchanted Moors, who sat grim and motionless, glaring upon them with unwinking eyes. At length, struck with a sudden fear of some fancied noise, they both rushed up the staircase, tumbled over one another into the upper apartment, overturned and extinguished the waxen taper, and the pavement again closed with a thundering sound.

Filled with dismay, they did not pause until they had groped their way out of the tower, and beheld the stars shining through the trees. Then seating themselves upon the grass, they divided the spoil, determining to content themselves for the present with this mere skimming of the jars, but to return on some future night and drain them to the bottom. To make sure of each other's good faith, also, they divided the talismans between them, one retaining the scroll and the other the taper; this done, they set off with light hearts and well-lined pockets for Granada.

As they wended their way down the hill, the shrewd Moor whispered a word of counsel in the ear of the simple little water carrier.

"Friend Peregil," said he, "all this affair must be kept a profound secret until we have secured the treasure and conveyed it out of harm's way. If a whisper of it gets to the ear of the Alcalde we are undone!"

"Certainly!" replied the Gallego; "nothing can be more true."

"Friend Peregil," said the Moor, "you are a discreet man, and I have no doubt you can keep a secret; but—you have a wife—"

"She shall not know a word of it!" replied the little water carrier sturdily.

"Enough," said the Moor. "I depend upon thy discretion and thy promise."

4.

Never was promise more positive and sincere; but alas! what man can keep a secret from his wife?

Certainly not such a one as Peregil the water carrier, who was one of the most loving and tractable of husbands. On his return home he found his wife moping in a corner.

"Mighty well!" cried she, as he entered. "You've come at last; after rambling about until this hour of the night. I wonder you have not brought home another Moor as a housemate." Then, bursting into tears, she began to wring her hands and smite her breast. "Unhappy woman that I am!" exclaimed she. "What will become of me! My house stripped and plundered by lawyers and police; my husband a do-no-good who no longer brings home bread for his family, but goes rambling about, day and night, with infidel Moors. Oh, my children! My children! What will become of us? We shall all have to beg in the streets!"

Honest Peregil was so moved by the distress of his spouse that he could not help whimpering also. His heart was as full as his pocket, and not to be restrained. Thrusting his hand into the latter, he hauled forth three or four broad gold pieces. The poor woman stared with astonishment, and could not understand the meaning of this golden shower. Before she could recover her surprise, the little Gallego drew forth a chain of gold and dangled it before her.

"Holy Virgin protect us!" exclaimed the wife. "What hast thou been doing, Peregil? Surely thou hast not been committing murder and robbery!"

The idea scarce entered the brain of the poor woman than it became a certainty with her. She saw a prison and a gallows in the distance, and a little bandy-legged Gallego dangling pendant from it; and, overcome by the horrors conjured up by her imagination, fell into violent hysterics.

What could the poor man do? He had no other means of pacifying his wife and dispelling the phantoms of her fancy, than by relating the whole story of his good fortune. This, however, he did not do until he had exacted from her the most solemn promise to keep it a profound secret from every living being.

To describe her joy would be impossible. She flung her arms round the neck of her husband, and almost strangled him with her caresses.

"Now, wife!" exclaimed the little man with honest exultation, "what say you now to the Moor's legacy? Henceforth never abuse me for helping a fellow creature in distress."

The honest Gallego retired to his sheepskin mat, and slept as soundly as if on a bed of down. Not so his wife. She emptied the whole contents of his pockets upon the mat, and sat all night counting gold pieces of Arabic coin, trying on necklaces and earrings, and fancying the figure she should one day make when permitted to enjoy her riches.

On the following morning the honest Gallego took a broad golden coin to a jeweler's shop to offer it for sale; pretending to have found it among the

ruins of the Alhambra. The jeweler saw that it had
an Arabic inscription and was of the purest gold;
he offered, however, but a third of its value, with
which the water carrier was perfectly content.
Peregil now bought new clothes for his little flock,
and all kinds of toys, together with ample provi-
sions for a hearty meal, and returning to his dwelling set all his children dancing around him, while
he capered in their midst, the happiest of fathers.

The wife of the water carrier kept her promise
of secrecy with surprising strictness. For a whole
day and a half she went about with a look of mystery and a heart swelling almost to bursting, yet
she held her peace, though surrounded by her
gossips. It is true she could not help giving herself
a few airs, apologized for her ragged dress, and
talked of ordering a new one all trimmed with
gold lace, and a new lace mantilla. She threw out
hints of her husband's intention of leaving his
trade of water carrying, as it did not altogether
agree with his health. In fact she thought they
should all retire to the country for the summer so
that the children might have the benefit of the
mountain air, for there was no living in the city
in this sultry season.

The neighbors stared at each other, and thought
the poor woman had lost her wits, and her airs and
graces and elegant pretensions were the theme of
universal scoffing and merriment among her
friends, the moment her back was turned.

If she restrained herself abroad, however, she indemnified herself at home, and, putting a string of rich oriental pearls round her neck, Moorish bracelets on her arms, an aigrette of diamonds on her head, sailed backwards and forwards in her slatternly rags about the room, now and then stopping to admire herself in a piece of broken mirror. Nay, in the impulse of her simple vanity, she could not resist on one occasion showing herself at the window, to enjoy the effect of her finery on the passers-by.

As the fates would have it, Pedrillo Pedrugo, the meddlesome barber, was at this moment sitting idly in his shop on the opposite side of the street, when his ever-watchful eye caught the sparkle of a diamond. In an instant he was at his loophole, reconnoitering the slattern spouse of the water carrier, decorated with the splendor of an Eastern bride. No sooner had he taken an accurate inventory of her ornaments than he posted off with all speed to the Alcalde. In a little while the hungry policeman was again on the scent, and before the day was over, the unfortunate Peregil was again dragged into the presence of the judge.

5.

"How is this, villain!" cried the Alcalde in a furious voice. "You told me that the infidel who died in your house left nothing behind but an empty coffer, and now I hear of your wife flaunting in her rags decked out with pearls and diamonds. Wretch, that thou art! Prepare to render up the spoils of thy miserable victim, and to swing on the gallows that is already tired of waiting for thee."

The terrified water carrier fell on his knees, and made a full relation of the marvelous manner in which he had gained his wealth. The Alcalde, the policeman, and the inquisitive barber listened with greedy ears to this Arabian tale of enchanted treasure. The policeman was dispatched to bring the Moor who had assisted in the incantation. The Moslem entered half frightened out of his wits at finding himself in the hands of the harpies of the law. When he beheld the water carrier standing with sheepish look and downcast countenance, he comprehended the whole matter. "Miserable animal," said he, as he passed near him, "did I not warn thee against babbling to thy wife?"

The story of the Moor coincided exactly with that of his colleague; but the Alcalde affected to be slow of belief, and threw out menaces of imprisonment and rigorous investigation.

"Softly, good Señor Alcalde," said the Mussulman, who by this time had recovered his usual shrewdness and self-possession. "Let us not mar fortune's favors in the scramble for them. Nobody knows anything of this matter but ourselves; let us keep the secret. There is wealth enough in the cave to enrich us all. Promise a fair division, and all shall be produced; refuse, and the cave shall remain forever closed."

The Alcalde consulted apart with his officer. The latter was an old fox in his profession.

"Promise anything," said he, "until you get possession of the treasure. You may then seize upon the whole, and if he and his accomplice dare to murmur, threaten them with the faggot and the stake as infidels and sorcerers."

The Alcalde relished the advice. Smoothing his brow and turning to the Moor, "This is a strange story," said he, "and may be true, but I must have proof of it. This very night you must repeat the incantation in my presence. If there be really such treasure, we will share it amicably between us, and say nothing further of the matter. If you have deceived me, expect no mercy at my hands. In the meantime you must remain in custody."

The Moor and that water carrier cheerfully agreed to these conditions, satisfied that the event would prove the truth of their words.

Toward midnight the Alcalde sallied forth secretly, attended by his officer and the meddlesome barber, all strongly armed. They conducted the Moor and the water carrier as prisoners, and were provided with the stout donkey of the latter, to bear off the expected treasure. They arrived at the tower without being observed, and tying the donkey to a fig tree, descended into the fourth vault of the tower.

The scroll was produced, the yellow waxen taper lighted, and the Moor read the form of incantation. The earth trembled as before, and the pavement opened with a thundering sound, disclosing the narrow flight of steps. The Alcalde, the policeman, and the barber were struck aghast, and could not summon courage to descend. The Moor and the water carrier entered the lower vault and found the two Moors seated as before, silent and motionless. They removed two of the great jars, filled with golden coin and precious stones. The water carrier bore them up one by one upon his shoulders, but though a strong-backed little man, and accustomed to carry burdens, he staggered beneath their weight, and found, when slung on each side of his donkey, they were as much as the animal could bear.

"Let us be content for the present," said the Moor. "Here is as much treasure as we can carry off without being perceived, and enough to make us all wealthy to our hearts' desire."

"Is there more treasure remaining behind?" demanded the Alcalde.

"The greatest prize of all," said the Moor; "a huge coffer, bound with bands of steel, and filled with pearls and precious stones."

"Let us have up the coffer by all means," cried the grasping Alcalde.

"I will descend for no more," said the Moor doggedly. "Enough is enough for a reasonable man; more is superfluous."

"And I," said the water carrier, "will bring up no further burden to break the back of my poor donkey."

Finding commands, threats, and entreaties equally vain, the Alcalde turned to his two adherents. "Aid me," said he, "to bring up the coffer, and its contents shall be divided between us." So saying, he descended the steps, followed, with trembling reluctance, by the policeman and the barber.

No sooner did the Moor behold them fairly earthed than he extinguished the yellow taper: the pavement closed with its usual crash, and the three worthies remained buried inside.

He then hastened up the different flights of steps, nor stopped until in the open air. The little water carrier followed him as fast as his short legs would permit.

"What have you done?" cried Peregil, as soon as he could recover his breath. "The Alcalde and the other two are shut up in the vault!"

"It is the will of Allah!" said the Moor devoutly.

"And will you not release them?" demanded the Gallego.

"Allah forbid!" replied the Moor, smoothing his beard. "It is written in the book of fate that they shall remain enchanted until some future adventurer shall come to break the charm. The will of Allah be done!" So saying, he hurled the end of the waxen taper far among the gloomy thickets of the glen.

There was no remedy; so the Moor and the water carrier proceeded with the richly laden donkey toward the city; nor could honest Peregil refrain from hugging and kissing his long-eared fellow-laborer, thus restored to him from the clutches of the law. And, in fact, it is doubtful which gave the simple-hearted little man most joy at the moment, the gaining of the treasure or the recovery of the donkey.

The two partners in good luck divided their spoil amicably and fairly, except that the Moor, who had a little taste for trinketry, made out to get into his heap most of the pearls and precious stones, and other baubles, but then he always gave the water carrier in lieu magnificent jewels of massy gold four times the size, with which the latter was heartily content. They took care not to linger within reach of accidents, but made off to enjoy their wealth undisturbed in other countries. The Moor returned into Africa, to his native city of Tetuan, and the Gallego, with his wife, his children, and his donkey, made their way to Portugal. Here, under the admonition and tuition of his wife, he became a personage of some consequence, for she made the little man array his long body and short legs in doublet and hose, with a feather in his hat and a sword by his side; and, laying aside the familiar appellation of Peregil, assume the more sonorous title of Don Pedro Gil. His progeny grew up a thriving and merry-hearted, though short and bandy-legged generation; while

the Senora Gil, be-fringed, be-laced, and be-tas-
seled from her head to her heels, with glittering
rings on every finger, became a model of slatternly
fashion and finery.

As to the Alcalde, and his adjuncts, they remained shut up under the great tower of the
Seven Floors, and there they remain spellbound to
the present day.